THE
END

A SHORT STORY COLLECTION

B. D. WEST

ISBN: 978-1-7370178-4-4

Any references to historical events, real people, or real places are used fictitiously. Names, characters, and places are products of the author's imagination.

Cover design by: ebooklaunch.com

Contents

Authorbdwest.com

This book is lovingly dedicated to my husband, friend, and strength, Eric Johnson. If it hadn't been for your encouragement, I never could have found the courage to write The End. I would also like to thank my son Dakota for all the inspiration and support you give me every single day. I want to express my gratitude to all my readers for accompanying me on this journey and for reading my wild stories. I look forward to sharing more adventures with you all.

Are writers created, or are they born? I feel as if I were born with a typewriter in my hands and a story on my lips. But I can't help but wonder if I am the author of the stories or have the stories taken control of me? It seems like I'm starting to lose my grip on what's real.

~Arthur Nightingale

Prologue

Arthur didn't know how long he had been sitting at his desk. He needed to write something - a short story, a novel, or even a novella. The pressure was on for him to write the next bestseller, with his wife, publisher, and fans all pushing him. Arthur had dominated the New York bestseller list for a decade, graced numerous writing magazine covers, delivered speeches at universities, libraries, and conventions, and even had discussions about a film based on one of his stories. It was the ideal life that every writer envisioned when they completed their debut novel.

His upper lip glistened with sweat as weakness took hold, and his hands trembled. Arthur felt his stomach cramp and churn with nausea. The situation was dire, and he desperately needed a drink. Despite his efforts to avoid becoming like his father, he now struggled to write a sentence without a drink. Getting sober couldn't have happened at a worse moment. How could anyone expect him to not take a drink after his mother died? His mouth was as dry as a desert. Arthur rubbed his chest as the heavy loneliness from his loss ached like a heart attack.

Understanding the struggles of authors is something few can grasp. Arthur questioned whether his fans believed he woke up, took the kids to school, returned home, made coffee, and effortlessly wrote a few chapters - it's never that simple. The truth was, he woke up, consumed pain reliever powders for the hangover, hastily drank scalding hot coffee, escorted the kids to school, and returned to the house. It became a weird mind game of how long Arthur could stare at the computer screen before giving up and playing on his social media until it was time to pick up the kids again from school. Occasionally, he would write a chapter, but most of the time, he felt like a fraud pretending to be extraordinary. Guilt and shame consumed Arthur. He would lie to Clare about his writing progress, even though he could tell she had her doubts. Admitting his daily failures was out of the question for him.

Writer's block felt like a sickness he couldn't find a cure for. People on the internet posed as experts, claiming to have the remedy for writer's block, but it was merely a marketing tactic to sell books or gain a larger social media following. The self-proclaimed experts failed to say anything he didn't already know. Arthur wanted a book that told him how to stop feeling like hell in the mornings, how to stop drinking, and how to keep going after a loss. He longed for someone to show him the way to find meaning in his life again.

Arthur kept a stack of notebooks with story ideas for when he needed fresh material to work on. Writer's block wasn't a problem for Arthur when it came to the story; it was the ending that was blocked.

None of the stories he wrote were complete. The loss of Arthur's mother upended his world- he couldn't bear the idea of writing a final ending.

The worlds he brought to life transformed into a prison he could not break free from.

The Lake

ON HIS WORN FRONT porch, Atticus sat in his favorite rocking chair with his coffee cup hovering near his lips. The morning heat was a clear indication of a scorching hot day ahead. It wasn't the typical reasons that made him hate summer, but something entirely different. The summer heat brought out the darkness hidden within people, which Atticus despised. It was as if the heat made it unbearable for people to hold the grudges, harsh words, resentment, financial troubles, and domestic hatred in the little room inside their minds where people control their impulses. The arrival of cooler weather allowed for easier containment of the evil within its human prison.

Atticus savored the slow burn of his coffee as it journeyed from his mouth to his throat. According to his mother, drinking hot coffee in the summer would provide cooling effects throughout the day. Despite it being untrue, Atticus found solace in remembering his mother that way. On mornings such as this one, Atticus thought of his parents in the very home he now enjoyed. The tiny white house with a crooked white picket fence housed five children, two dogs, and a scrappy black cat with a bad attitude. Atticus never felt the house was crowded, even though he had shared a room and bed with his four siblings. He never felt poor, even though they rarely bought anything from the stores in town. He only realized his financial difference when he attended school with non-farm kids who teased him relentlessly. They teased him about his blue jean overalls, the metal bucket he used for his school lunch, and the shoes that had holes in them. It appeared that nothing about him was off-limits for teasing, causing his anger to escalate like a raging inferno.

When asked why they couldn't just buy their food in town, his father would take the rag from his back pocket, wipe his brow, and say, "The good Lord provided us with the land, we will do our part to make it thrive. He gives us what we need, boy. Don't you forget that. Count your blessings." Atticus could vividly recall how the summer heat would intensify his anger when his father spoke those words. He didn't dare sass his father. He was a hardworking man who always tried his best to support his family. There was never a time when Atticus went hungry, felt cold, or experienced a lack of love in his home.

Looking out at the expanse of vibrant green grass, Atticus couldn't help but smile, remembering his father's tireless efforts on this very land. Atticus decided to attend college and study law instead of focusing on farming, which wasn't his strength. The decision to move to Nashville, Tennessee after he received his law degree, was one he regretted; it was quite a change from his small Kentucky town. Following his father's sudden heart attack, Atticus returned home to Deer Hollow. Overwhelmed by grief, his mother eventually passed away due to a broken heart. Each of his four brothers had no desire to inherit the farm; consequently, they all left and never gave it a second thought. Atticus couldn't blame them too much; Kentucky didn't hold much for those who wanted more than a relaxed lifestyle.

His reminiscing was interrupted by the sound of tires crunching on the gravel in his driveway. Atticus sighed deeply as he peered into his almost empty mug. On his day off, he made it clear that he could only be bothered by an emergency or a death. The worries of fifty men were evident on Deputy Green's face. Atticus sensed that his arrival was a harbinger of bad news.

Deputy Green parked the police cruiser in front of Atticus's worn-out blue porch. Anxiously, he opened the door on the driver's side and stepped out. With sweat streaming down his face, he glanced around the farm's property. "They were right, no doubt about it. It's beautiful out here." When he looked at Atticus, his smile disappeared from his face. "Sheriff Hightower, I know you specifically mentioned not to disturb you unless there was a death, but..."

"Someone dead?" Atticus cut in.

Stuttering slightly, the Deputy continued, "Um, no, sir. I..."

"Then why am I seeing your sweaty mug on this fine morning? My day off, I might add." Atticus knew he wasn't doing his best to hide his annoyance, but this had been the first day off he had in over two months, and his patience had dwindled down to almost nothing because of sleep deprivation and the heat. The summer heat had reached its peak and was fighting to stay alive. Summer seemed to have a mind of its own as fall quickly approached. It fiercely battled to cling onto its remaining time with a determination to bring misery upon the people of Deer Hollow.

Deputy Green could see the anger building on Atticus's face. He chose not to be intimidated by the expression on the Sheriff's face. It was essential for him to be there, and he intended to carry out his responsibilities. Steadying himself, the Deputy walked towards the steps on the porch. "Sheriff Hightower, I apologize for the interruption, but this is crucial. We've got ourselves a situation at Deerfield Lake."

"What sort of situation? Is it a, I have time for another cup of coffee and a shower situation or deep crap situation?"

"Deep crap, sir."

Atticus let out another sigh as he tilted his head to the side and gave a nod. "Aren't they planning to drain the lake this week?"

Deputy Green nodded his head. "They already drained the lake, sir, and what they stumbled upon is something I don't think we were ever meant to find."

"Great; is the media there?"

"It hasn't happened yet, but I don't believe we can keep this under control much longer."

Disbelievingly, Atticus shook his head. "Have we got a body?"

"Negative, sir. We've got bodies."

Nothing more needed to be said. Atticus went inside his house to change into his official attire as the Deputy waited inside of the police cruiser. Deputy Green tried his best not to show his surprise when he saw the Sheriff in uniform and ready to leave in such a timely manner. Sheriff Hightower, despite being sixty, was anything but slow. As Atticus settled into the passenger seat, he casually grabbed a pair of aviator sunglasses and put them on. "Let's go." Deputy Green gave a slight nod as he started up the cruiser and pulled away from the little white farmhouse.

The shade trees that ran alongside the dirt road to Deerfield Lake offered little relief from the heat. The radio's temperature gage read ninety degrees, while the clock showed eleven in the morning. Atticus responded with an eye roll. It would only get hotter as the day rolled on, and that spelled disaster for a body baking in the sun. Skipping breakfast didn't seem like a great idea until that thought rolled through his mind. Atticus hoped his morning coffee wouldn't pull a rebellion.

Deerfield Lake, which used to be a lake but now is a muddy mess, came into sight. The entire fleet of police cruisers from the department was parked at the soggy edges of the lake. Upon seeing Atticus and Deputy Green pull in behind them, the police officers on the scene turned to watch them. When Atticus stepped out of the car, his view was filled with nothing but wet dirt and police officers, causing concern to creep in. His brand-new shoes were on the verge of being ruined by the mud. The police officers parted like the red sea as Atticus approached the banks of Deerfield Lake.

While his mind grasped the dreadful secret the lake had concealed, he could sense the eyes fixed on his back. Atticus shielded his eyes from the sun's light by raising his hand to his brow. Swallowing hard, he fought to suppress a newfound fear that was unraveling. The skeletal remains of countless bodies protruded from the mud. Under the layers of sediment, some remains were barely visible, while others belonged to those who fought for their lives. The stairs, which were all that remained of a foundation, were draped with the remains of people. Among all the bodies, one stood out to Atticus. It looked like the body of an adult laying on top of a juvenile. The child was being embraced by the adult skeleton, with its arms wrapped around protectively. The lake was silent and still. Several of the bodies had empty eye sockets looking towards the sky while others lay twisted with contorted boney expressions.

As Deputy Green approached him, Atticus felt a lump forming in his throat. "What do you make of this, Sheriff?"

Atticus coughed to clear his throat. "It's time for us to pick up the phone and start dialing."

"Who do you want me to call?"

"Everyone. Before you do that, form a perimeter around the lake, and block off the entrance to every access road. We need to hold off on making any statements or allowing the press to access the lake until we have more information about what the hell is happening here. Get Sarah on the phone. I want her to research this lake. I want to know everything. Who built it, who flooded it... everything she can dig up. Tell her to step on it. The public is going to want answers."

Deputy Green's reply was barely audible to Atticus as he departed to carry out his instructions. The possibilities of what could have happened were swirling in his mind. The visible remnants of buildings and homes in the mud suggested a town. There was an eerie sense of foreboding in the air. The lake seemed to have a story for Atticus, but death's barriers prevented it from being told. A tale of agony, lost voices, and suffering yearned to be told by the lake. Atticus felt chills creeping up and down his spine as memories of fishing trips and swimming in the lake's waters flooded his mind, unaware of the eyes watching from below. What was once a lively town had transformed into a desolate wasteland of mud.

Knowing he would regret it later, Atticus decided to get a closer look. He briefly mourned the loss of his new shoes and took a step forward. A rush of cold, damp mud slid up to his right knee. With a deep breath, Atticus sank his left foot into the mud. It felt like a suction pulling his leg deep into the mire. He frequently used the phrase of feeling like he was trudging uphill in knee-deep sludge, but this was a whole new level of difficulty. With each stride he made, the mud altered its shape and filled his footwear. The frigid slush oozed through his socks, finding its way between each toe. Atticus felt as if the mud was fighting against him. It felt like the lake was urging him to sink into the damp earth with the corpses.

As Atticus ventured deeper into the buried town, he started experiencing an unsettling sensation. Atticus couldn't discern if he was having an anxiety attack or if his mind was playing tricks on him. The faces of the bodies began to turn toward him, the sky darkened, and the ground beneath him vibrated. He felt his lungs constrict, making it difficult to breathe. A powerful force started dragging him forward. Atticus realized that if he didn't make it back to solid ground, he would face death. With his head heavy as lead, he turned slightly to catch a glimpse of the shoreline. Atticus had the sensation of looking through a spyglass, distorting and warping his perception of everything. The trees surrounding the lake seemed to bend forward, as if they were being pulled into the murky burial ground. Atticus wanted to yell out for help, but his voice felt dried up. For a moment, he shut his eyes and directed his attention to his breathing. With each tremor, Atticus's determination became more steadfast. He realized that stepping into fresh mud would be fatal, so he took precautions by lifting his feet one at a time and retraced his steps in reverse. Skeletal hands reached out to him as they asked for the help he could not give them. In his desperate struggle for survival, his soul was shattered by the piercing wails and moans. With each step he took, the world around him drew nearer and the souls of the lost began to fade. The last step brought everything into focus on the bank.

Atticus, exhausted and breathless, bent over and closed his eyes, placing his hand over his heart while taking a deep breath of the fresh air. Running towards Atticus, Deputy Green placed his hand on his shoulder. "Sheriff Hightower! Where did you come from?"

Atticus felt confused as perspiration soaked his uniform. "What?"

It was Deputy Green's turn to feel confused. "Sir, are you alright?"

The earth felt as if was becoming more real the longer he stood there with the officer. "I'm fine. Why are you asking me that?"

"Sir?"

Atticus felt a surge of anger as he straightened up and opened his eyes. Fear gripped Atticus as he observed the enveloping darkness. Above him, the stars shimmered while the moon illuminated the sky like a lantern. He directed his gaze downward onto the lakebed. Among the mud and crumbled foundations, the remains were covered by an eerie glow from the moon and mist. The trees and roots, with their twisted and bare branches, appeared like skeletal fingers reaching towards the heavens. It was enough to make Atticus want to run, but he couldn't. All he could do was inhale the chilly, musty air permeated with the scent of rotting plants and corpses. Atticus turned his gaze towards the Deputy. His voice quivered as he spoke. "What did you ask me?"

"Um, I asked if you were alright."

Atticus made an impatient gesture with his hand. "No, before that."

Deputy Green seemed confused, unsure if the Sheriff was testing him or if he had gone insane. "I asked where you had come from."

Atticus glanced around one last time, taking in the darkness that surrounded him. He couldn't help but notice his voice sounded like a ghost. "How long was I gone?"

Deputy Green checked the time on his watch. "It's ten o'clock, sir. Everyone has been looking for you."

"That's impossible." Atticus responded, speaking more to himself than to the Deputy. "I think it's best if I go home now."

As he sank into his beloved rocking chair, Atticus watched the police cruiser's red taillights vanish into the night. He couldn't make sense of what had taken place or how he had lost the last eleven hours. Is it possible that he disappeared after entering the mud? Throughout his career as an officer turned sheriff, Atticus had encountered numerous things, but nothing as bizarre as this had occurred before. In his long career in Kentucky, he had encountered an uncountable number of remains, yet none of them ever stared at him like the lake's corpses did, nor did they make an attempt on his life.

A sunrise painted a picture-perfect farmland scene. Atticus was wide awake all night. He spent half the night questioning all that he witnessed and the other half of the night and into the morning questioning his entire existence. He couldn't feel his legs, and his arms were chilled by the morning breeze. He needed to move before his body wove itself into the wood of his chair. As he stood to stretch, a fire red Porsche flew down his driveway and came to a screeching halt in front of Atticus's house. With a stack of papers in hand, Sarah leaped out of her car. "Atticus, you won't believe what I found!" Sarah exclaimed, out of breath, as she slammed her car door shut.

A smile spread across Atticus's face. Sarah's drive and enthusiasm added excitement to his job. "Come on in and tell me."

Sarah trailed after Atticus as he entered the house and eagerly observed him bustling around the kitchen, preparing coffee. He gestured towards a seat at the table. "Would you like a cup? If I look half as scrambled as you do, we are both going to need a boost to get through the rest of the day."

"I know I look a mess, but I was up digging through the archives all night. It's not an easy task to do in that old, musty basement. I promise you, they're growing mushrooms down there," she said, letting out a tired giggle. "It took me until I reached the last box to find this little gem."

Atticus handed Sarah a cup of coffee and then took a seat with his own cup across from her. "What's in here?" he asked, opening the aged file and flipping through the pages.

"That, good sir, is documents from nineteen twenty-nine. Before Deerfield Lake was a lake, it was the town of Hartsville. Although not the wealthiest town in history, the land was in high demand. The railroad and affluent travelers quickly recognized the value of the farmland and picturesque hills. The intention was to create a resort in Deer Hollow, but Hartsville opposed the idea. There was a man by the name of Harold Gray. He was some big honcho for the railroad, and he tried to reason with the townspeople of Hartsville. His attempt to bribe them with money failed."

Atticus shook his head. "Damn railroads. They always leave a trail of blood behind them. So, what did he do next?"

"If you look at page three, you'll find documentation of his legal action against them. Turns out the Judge ruled in Mr. Gray's favor. After reading the notes from the trial, I'm guessing that the judge was in his back pocket. Following the trial, police reports indicated that the townspeople declined payment and disregarded evacuation warnings. This went on for at least a year. The judge responsible for the cruel decision died of a heart attack, and a new judge stepped in."

Atticus carefully studied the papers laid out in front of him. "His name was Judge Stone."

Sarah nodded her head. "Yeah, that's the name. Well, if you look in his notes after Mr. Gray came calling, he refused to enforce the last judge's ruling. It continued for over a year. After nineteen thirty-two the paper trail goes cold. I refused to believe that was the end of the story, so I continued moving boxes and discovered a briefcase hidden behind an old desk. And I found this." Sarah reached into her oversized purse and pulled out a small leather diary. "This diary belonged to Judge

Stone. Most of it was just private thoughts on old cases, but when I got to the back, I nearly died!"

Atticus grabbed the diary and opened it. The adhesive properties of the old ink caused some of the pages to stick together. Upon turning to the last page, he was hit by the smell of aging and mildewed paper. Before diving into the text, he locked eyes with Sarah, whose blue eyes were filled with anticipation. With a downward glance, Atticus directed his attention to the paper and began to read.

> *I won't be making any more entries after this one. I have faith that it will be uncovered some-day, and that justice will be served to those who caused my death. I've been poisoned by Mr. Gray, the Kentucky railroad, and their as-sociates. With my last ounce of strength, I write these words as I cling to life. Whoever you are, please take this journal and find someone who can keep my family safe. I don't know which wicked person contaminated my medicine, but I'm afraid I won't live to see tomorrow to find out. I want it to be known that I tried to help the people of Hartsville. I uncovered a most sinister plot to flood Hartsville, and I foolishly confronted Mr. Gray. I received what I believed to be empty threats, so I wrote a letter to the governor. With my imminent demise, I fear my letter has been intercepted or the governor is part of this vile conspiracy. Mr. Gray is the devil. I firmly believe in this fact. His plan is to use the dam water to wipe out the entire town, and I don't have the power to rescue them. I*

implore you, as a person of honor, to protect my
wife, Martha.

Atticus lifted his eyes from the diary to look at Sarah. "Those people were completely blindsided. The railroad opened the dam and drowned a whole town like rats. What kind of monster would have done something like that?"

Sarah shrugged her shoulders. "Maybe Judge Stone was right. Maybe Harold was the devil. The worst part of the story is the fact the railroad never came to this area, and the rich people never built their precious resort; it was all for nothing."

Was Judge Stone right? Did the devil show up in Deer Hollow to massacre the entire town of Hartsville? Where was Harold Gray and what happened to Judge Stone's wife? Did she escape, or was she lying among the remains of Hartsville? Atticus's head began to pound. This was a story that needed to be brought into the light for all to see. Would the railroad finally see its day in court for the murder of over one thousand souls?

Atticus couldn't say for certain if he could find justice for the victims of Hartsville, but something told him the lake wouldn't rest until it claimed him as well.

Parasomnia

GINA GAZED DOWNWARD, FIXATING on her own feet. Her shoes were the newest thing she owned. Despite being bought second-hand at a thrift store, they still had the original store's tag on them. She purchased the running sneakers, hoping they had never been worn. They were a puke brown with white stripes. Her decision to buy them was because they pinched her feet. The shoes kept her distracted from the eyes staring at her. Gina despised being the center of attention. It made her feel self-conscience about everything. She knew she was being judged for her style of clothing, the food she ate or didn't eat, how skinny she was, and they even picked on her for how short her hair was. When her family discovered she had cut her hair and dyed it fire-red, it became the hot topic in town. Her family didn't bother hiding their ill intentions anymore and implied she was crazy in every conversation they had with her.

Encouraged by her mother to seek help, Gina sat opposite the psychologist, who awaited a response she couldn't provide. Dr. Williams was the type of woman Gina felt she could never relate to. With her golden locks, beauty, and heavenly fragrance, she was irresistible. She had the perfect hourglass figure that made her body look flawless. Dr. Williams always coordinated her outfits with the weather. When it was chilly, she would don a wool jacket in fall hues, paired with a curve-hugging skirt. During the summer, she wore a vibrant yellow silk blouse paired with blue pants and yellow high heels. Not once was there a day when a single strand of her hair was disheveled.

"Gina, are you still with me?" Dr. William's voice sent shockwaves through Gina.

Gina raised her gaze slowly. She traced the trail from Dr. Williams' black pumps to her legs, which were adorned with shiny pantyhose as they intertwined. Her gaze then moved to her fall orange skirt and black coat before she replied. "I don't know how to answer you."

As she twirled her fountain pen, Dr. Williams nodded in understanding. "Are they here?"

Gina looked around the office- she saw nothing. "No."

"And why do you think that is?" Dr. Willliams said as she lifted the end of her pen to her perfectly painted lips. It was as if she thought chewing her pen made her look intelligent.

"Because you have your curtains open and it's daylight." Answering that question was a piece of cake.

"Does that keep them away?"

"What?"

Dr. Williams directed her pen towards the window, glancing in that direction. "The curtains. Does that make them stay away because they are open?"

With a hint of anger in her tone, Gina shook her head. She had already told the doctor a million times about the shadows. "No, it's the light. They only exist in the shadows."

"The shadow people?"

"Yes," Gina said, trying to hide her annoyance. It was a fact she had discussed many times: they were the people *of* the shadow, not shadow people.

In her typical condescending manner, Dr. Williams nodded her head once more. She couldn't hide the fact she thought Gina was full of it. The good doctor thought her face said, "I believe you." What her face actually said was, "You are nuts, and I'm stringing you along for money and for the paper I'm writing on you." Gina looked down at her feet again as the doctor asked more questions. "Do they ever talk to you?"

"I told you, they do sometimes. I just ignore them." Gina's eyes burned and her cheeks flushed.

"What do they say to you, Gina?"

With an eye roll, Gina answered. "They ask me if I can see them and sometimes, they ask me to go with them." Gina opted not to reveal the details, especially regarding the shadow man who frequented her window each night.

They lapsed into their usual silence as the doctor contemplated her next question. The heat from Gina's embarrassment made her sweat. "Where do they want you to go, Gina?"

Gina raised her eyes. "The land of shadow."

Dr. Williams nodded her head. "Gina, do you believe the land of shadow exists?"

Despite knowing she should say no, Gina couldn't fully convince herself that the land of shadow wasn't real. Nevertheless, she knew that she could never utter those words to the doctor. "I don't know."

"Is self-harm something you think about?" In a deceptive display of empathy, Dr. Williams tilted her head.

Gina felt a surge of anger and shame coursing through her body. "Absolutely not!" Gina shook her head in disgust while tapping her foot. Despite attending ten sessions, there was no improvement. A year later, she still hadn't made any progress towards getting a full night's sleep. Instead of feeling less crazy, she actually felt even crazier. "You think I'm out of my mind, don't you?" Gina watched as a play of emotions swept over the doctor's flawless face. It was evident that Dr. Williams was caught off guard by the unexpected outburst.

A curious feeling of satisfaction washed through her entire being. She didn't even wait for a response as she blurted out, "If you don't believe me, how can you help me?"

Dr. Williams's crimson-colored lips trembled as she fought to compose herself. Gina hoped to inflict some pain on her, or at least bruise her ego slightly, but she had no such luck as she responded calmly and composed. "Gina, I believe *you* believe they are real, and I am here to help you make them go away. You want to sleep, don't you?"

"Of course I want to sleep, but can't we at least entertain the notion they could be real? Perhaps there is a yet-to-be-discovered species of humans. I..."

Dr. Williams threw up her manicured hands and gently shook her head to stop Gina from completing her sentence. "Gina, you know it's not within the realm of possibility. The universe is devoid of any other beings besides us. There are no aliens."

"I'm not referring to extraterrestrial beings. Imagine if there was a species of beings that remain unknown to us. Are there individuals who go unnoticed until we're sleep deprived or not paying attention?" Gina replied.

"Gina, you will sleep again once you stop believing in this impossible notion." Dr. Williams took out her prescription pad and started writing. "I hope you will fill this prescription this time, Gina. It will help you sleep."

As it glided over the notepad, the pen shimmered in the sunlight. The sound of paper being ripped from the notepad sent shivers down Gina's spine. With a hint of reluctance, Gina accepted the paper and swiftly hid it away in her pocket. Absent-mindedly, she nodded, got up, put on her coat, and committed to scheduling another appointment. She came close to stopping at the front desk to make another appointment, but ultimately opted not to. Something about the secretary's look was off when she walked towards the desk. She had a look of complete amusement, and her face clearly said, "I know what you talk about and you're crazy." As she passed by, Gina gave her the same smile and exclaimed, "No need for another appointment; I'm cured!"

Not bothering to look back, Gina quickened her steps, hopped onto the elevator, and watched with satisfaction as she watched Dr. Williams come shooting out of her office. She had heard Gina's comments and tried to intervene. With a sarcastic gesture, Gina waved goodbye to both of them as the elevator doors shut. For the first time in two years, a laugh broke free from her lips. At first, it surprised her, but then she laughed once more, this time with even greater force. By the time the elevator doors opened on the first floor, Gina's stomach ached, and her cheeks hurt. Luckily, nobody was waiting outside the elevator doors to get on. Gina's pocket vibrated as her phone began to ring. It was her mom or the good doctor trying to talk her into going back; it wasn't going to happen.

When the day was over, Gina found herself in her cramped apartment, holding a glass of wine. The sun was almost completely set and the shadow man, as she came to call him, would show up like clockwork. He always refrained from entering her apartment whenever her lamps were still burning; instead, he would position himself outside the window, where it was the darkest. Tonight, Gina was going to confront him. It was the only way to make him go away. She was sure of that fact. Gina savored her wine, watching as the last of the daylight vanished behind the L.A. skyline. The streetlights and building lights switched on in perfect sync, creating a harmonious glow throughout the area. Looking at the clock on the wall, Gina knew the shadow man would be there any second; he was never late. There were nights when he would watch her by the window with curiosity, and then there were nights when he couldn't contain his impatience and paced around. At times, he would attempt to engage in conversation with her, but Gina would block him out by using her earbuds or cranking up the television.

One night, Gina placed a lamp in front of the window on purpose so he could not approach. The day after, Gina felt remorseful and promptly removed it, unsure of the reason. Three days passed before he came back. The shadow man appeared relieved, and honestly, Gina felt the same way. Oddly, she had become dependent on the shadow man's presence and felt a strange need for him to be around. Once her family and friends believed she was insane, Gina's world turned into a solitary existence. There were days when she hoped someone would call or come by, even if it were to tell her she needed to be committed to a home. Gina thought it was odd that someone could desire companionship, or at least the sound of another person's voice, even if it was a shadowy delusion.

Right on schedule, the shadow man showed up. A combination of fear and excitement made Gina's heart flutter. She had never approached him before, but she was doing it now. As she moved closer, the shadow man instinctively took a step back. Gina reached out and opened the window. Turning around, she proceeded to turn off every lamp in her apartment, then faced the curious stare of the shadow man. "Can you enter my home?"

With suspicion, the shadowy figure surveyed the area, but ultimately took a chance. Without making a sound, his transparent shape glided over the windowsill and into the apartment. Gina observed as his pale blue eyes roamed around her apartment, eventually fixing their gaze on her. With a cautious tone, his voice was both gentle and strong. "Thank you."

Tremors ran through Gina's entire body as her mind raced. Maintaining her composure, she took a deep breath and asked, "For what?"

"Trusting me."

The answer he gave her wasn't what she expected, and she had doubts about trusting him. "Are you able to sit down?"

The shadow man directed his gaze towards a chair that was close by. Gina watched as he chose her grandmother's blue overstuffed chair. "I can." Quietly and with caution, he lowered himself into a sitting position. It was as if he were afraid that he would either break the chair or make too much noise. Gina grabbed her wineglass. As she poured herself another glass of wine, her hands trembled. As he watched her closely, the shadow man uttered. "Do I make you nervous?"

While pouring the wine, Gina let out a sarcastic laugh. "I'm indulging in a glass of wine while conversing with one of my delusions. So, yeah, I think I am a bit nervous. It's not every day a gal goes insane."

"There is no need to be. You have nothing to fear from me, and I'm not a figment of your imagination."

Before responding, Gina took a big gulp from her glass. "Everyone thinks I am crazy. After this, I think I may just be."

"Your kind has always been so cynical and full of doubt," the shadow man said matter of fact.

"Our kind?" Gina asked, showing her confusion.

The man with the shadowy silhouette gestured towards the couch. "Please sit." Gina did as she was asked and waited for the shadow man to continue. "Yes, your kind. We are similar, you and I."

Gina's eyebrows lifted on her forehead. "Indeed?"

"You're still not convinced that I exist?"

"I'm not sure of anything. It's possible that you are a tumor in my brain, or maybe I'm confined to a bed in a mental facility, and you are a result of electric shock therapy. My mother did mention that she would have me institutionalized. It is possible she succeeded." Gina replied.

The shadow man's lips curved into an amused smile. In a spectral manner, he possessed a handsome charm. "Gina, I am just as real as you are."

When he uttered her name, Gina felt cold chills spill over her arms. "Why are you bothering me? I've been sleepless for a year, and you refuse to go away. Why?"

"I'm sorry for the stress I've caused you. I've tried to engage in conversation with you, but you chose to ignore me." The ghostly hands of the shadowy figure clutched the worn upholstery of his seat. "You need to come with me."

Gina felt a tightening in her throat. "Where?" she asked, fully aware of the answer.

"My world."

Not knowing why, Gina had to ask a question that had been burning since this figure showed up. "What is your name?"

Once again, the mysterious man's dark face revealed a smile. "I go by the name Lark."

Gina nodded her head. "Well, Lark, I cannot come with you. I don't know you, nor do I trust you. You are a weird apparition that is haunting me and if I can get a few nights' sleep, I think you will cease to exist."

In response, Lark leaned forward and pleaded with Gina, "Don't make me leave. It was destiny for us to have met. Have you considered how rare it is for your species to come across individuals like us? Most humans only see us for a brief second when they have missed an hour or two of sleep. They catch sight of us as we walk by their window or doorway from the corner of their eye, but they disregard our existence. Gina, you possess a unique quality that sets you apart."

"Others have caught a glimpse of you, huh? It's not just me? If others have seen you, how can I be considered special?"

"We've been seen by others, but only fleetingly. Out of everyone I've encountered, you're the only human who can see me for extended periods. It must mean something. Come back with me."

Gina shook her head. "I can't do that. That's insane. I can't just leave."

Standing up, Lark started to pace around. "I know you don't know me, except for seeing me outside of your window. I know how things must seem to you, but I have a gut feeling you are meant to come with me. Can't you sense it as well?"

Despite the reasons being unknown, Gina was certain that Lark believed in what he was saying. She felt crazy for entertaining this shadowy figure, but what was the alternative? Everyone thought she was crazy anyway, and she had already come this far. What kind of life was she living? It was a half-life, if you could even call it that; every day was the same. Gina followed the monotonous routine of getting out of bed, making coffee, going to work part-time at the library, and returning home every evening, rinse and repeat.

Rising from her seat, Gina walked towards the window. Behind her, Lark's pacing abruptly ceased. While she admired the twinkling city lights in the distance, she could feel his gaze on her back. A hot California breeze drifted through her window. "Lark, what if I'm completely bonkers? What if none of this is real? What happens if you're not real?"

Lark moved closer to Gina and stood beside her. "Can you convince me you are real?"

Gina let out a halfhearted chuckle. "I guess not."

"It is impossible for me to prove my existence to you, just as it is for you to prove yours to me. I just know that I am." Lark sighed. "Come with me, Gina."

Gina shifted her gaze to meet Lark's eyes. He mirrored her intensity with his own gaze, eager for her response. "When do we leave?"

Relief swept over Lark's face. His spectral body rose into the air and landed on the window's ledge. "Now; take my hand." Lark turned and held out his hand.

It never crossed Gina's mind until that moment if she could physically touch Lark's hand. She could see right through him, yet he confidently held out his hand as if he could be touched. The instant her hand met his, and she stepped onto the windowsill, a wave of warmth surged through her. A feeling of giddiness and happiness washed over her. It had been years since she last felt those emotions. Gina looked down at their hands intertwined and was shocked to see her hand was as dark and as transparent as Lark's. Holding her free hand in front of her face, she caught sight of Lark's surprised expression. "I'm a shadow," she said breathlessly.

"You're a shadow," Lark replied.

Gina didn't know if the land of shadow was a new plane of existence, her insanity, or death as she replied, "Lark, what does it mean?"

"It means I'm taking you home."

Gently, Lark took Gina's hand and guided her into the land of shadow.

The Game

WITH THE CAMERA PROVIDED by the game show, Jake secured the tripod. He had just enough time to record with the remaining daylight on Vancouver Island. Using the light on the camera was out of the question for him; the battery was almost dead. As the camera turned on, the red light started blinking, and the recording began. Jake cleared his throat. *"It's me, Jake, back again. I'm uncertain how long I can record before this battery dies. There's only one bar left, and it's blinking. I'm unsure why the crew hasn't come to give me a replacement battery as they promised, but I'll try to remember everything that occurs after this device loses power. I'm feeling a bit uneasy about the medics not stopping by, either. It's their usual routine to come by and check on me once a week. I must admit, I looked forward to their company. I'm unsure how long I have been here; I lost count at one hundred and five days. I made a foolish decision to keep my days recorded on an old log near the water over there. I didn't expect it to storm and wash away such a heavy piece of driftwood. But no sense in crying over spilled milk, I guess."*

Jake's stomach rumbled. *"I'm getting hungry; I don't have too much fat left to lose. I have to keep pushing forward for as long as I possibly can. How long that will be? I do not know."*

Jake gazed at his calloused hands, a testament to his twenty-seven years of work on the farm. Before this, his hands possessed an immense strength, but the relentless grip of hunger was wearing him down. Looking back at the camera that was blinking faster, Jake continued. *"I did my best to dry as much fish as I could and stored it beneath my shelter, but now I'm running low, and my gill net isn't working anymore. I believe the cold weather has forced the fish to go deeper into the water. It snowed last night, and it appears that there will be more snow tonight."* In disbelief, Jake shook his head. *"I can't believe I'm saying this but, if someone doesn't come soon to tell me I've won or that I am too sick to keep playing this game, I have to tap out."* The camera went dark.

Jake looked around; he had been on the island for at least three months, and now that the camera was dead, he felt completely isolated. The camera at least provided him with someone to talk to, and now he had been silenced. For several weeks, when he felt desperate, Jake would reach for the emergency walkie-talkie clipped to his belt. Just touching it, knowing they would come if he called to tap out, gave him a strange sense of comfort. Jake's hand shifted from the walkie-talkie to his breast pocket. Like an invisible shield, his family photo was there to protect him. Without even glancing at it, he knew his wife was gazing at the camera, beaming beside him while cradling their baby girl. He was playing the game for them- for the whole family. The farm hadn't been doing too well and Sarah was selling it while he was gone. The game's winnings could make starting over a little easier. It could mean so many worries would be gone.

Once he packed up the camera equipment, Jake made his way to the campsite. Although it was small, he felt proud of the setup. On the first day after the boat dropped him off on the shore, he found a boulder as tall as he was. To avoid exhausting himself, Jake kept the shelter simple and used sticks to prop up his tarp, placing them strategically around the front of the boulder. Once he had made sure they were secure, he covered the sticks and boulder with his tarp. It looked like an ancient hut, but it provided warmth and cover from the rain.

After placing the camera inside of his hut, Jake decided to start a fire. In his pot, he still had dried fish skins, seaweed, and mushrooms from when he first arrived on the island. Although it was mostly water, it would suffice as soup to get him through one more night. Jake wondered how much time the flint in his pocket had left. Every night for three months, he relied on it to start a fire, but it appeared to be losing its effectiveness. With each passing night, the challenge of generating a sizable spark grew more daunting. Jake arranged some pieces of dried wood into a triangle shape before taking some moss from his coat pocket he had found that morning and placed it under the logs. Afterward, he took out the flint and got to work. The flash of the flint temporarily illuminated the surrounding darkness. He tried to keep his mind on the job at hand and not on the blackened trees pressing in around him.

Fear of the dark was something Jake had never experienced. When you're raised on a farm, you become accustomed to the dark. Farmers woke up before sunrise and went to bed long after dark, but there was a house full of light to go home to when the day was done. There was an eerie feeling that accompanied the darkness on Vancouver Island, with no means of escape. It took several weeks to get used to the sounds of the night. Jake found it easy to get used to the rhythm of the wind blowing, or an occasional animal sound, but it was the other noises that sent chills down his spine. On some nights, Jake would wake up to the sound of twigs breaking or an unknown creature sniffing near his shelter. It was the crunching noise in the dark that made him question every life choice he ever made. The game restricted the use of weapons, allowing only hunting gear. Jake had brought a handmade bow and arrow for hunting, but he wasn't against breaking the rules to kill a bear or whatever monster that chose to eat his dinner so close to his shelter if he had to.

After many attempts, a spark emerged from the flint and landed on the moss. Jake bent down and blew on the small ember, trying to catch fire. He felt a wave of relief as the flame grew larger and consumed the logs. Once the flames died down, Jake positioned his pot of leftover fish near the fire to warm. This was the time Jake would usually talk to the camera, but the studio light the producers gave him stopped working, and the camera was now dead. The small amount of life left in his headlamp had to be saved for a moment of desperation. He felt stupid, but he saw the camera as his volleyball Wilson from that movie where the man was stranded on an island. Jake did not know how he could live without speaking another word until the medics came to check on him.

Jake noticed a piece of driftwood nearby and considered carving a face on it. To fill the silence, he could speak to it like the camera, simply to hear his own voice. Laughing to himself, Jake muttered, "I'm going insane. I can't believe it."

The sound of a loud snap made Jake's amusement fade away. Jake stood and placed his hand in front of the bright flames, using it to block the light as he tried to see over the fire. With narrowed eyes, Jake strained to see better as another loud crack echoed in the air. There was movement heading towards his campsite. The sound of the footsteps didn't match that of a bear, and there was no noticeable aroma in the blowing wind. You could usually detect the sour scent of bears and hear them huffing and snorting to indicate their presence. This was different. The sound resembled footsteps, but that seemed impossible. Jake strained even more. Could this be it? Was the game over? Were they here to tell him he had won or was his imagination playing with his senses? Jake decided to say something. "Hello?"

The pace of the footsteps grew faster. A bizarre thought came into Jake's mind. Imagine if this turned out to be a sasquatch or some other horrifying creature. Would it be there to eat him? Jake glanced at the bow resting by his shelter's entrance. He decided to leave it until he could see whatever was headed in his direction. "Hello, is anyone there?" Jake yelled once again.

This time, someone answered. "Hello?"

Fear caused Jake's heart to throb in his throat. He didn't think anyone would actually answer. "Yes? Hello? Can you see me?"

"Yes, hold on, I'm coming," said the disembodied voice.

With his eyes fixed on the tree line, Jake patiently awaited the appearance of someone, and eventually caught sight of him. From the woods emerged a man clad in a backpack and a heavy blue winter coat. His face, though dirty, wore a smile as his blond hair poked out like straw from under a knitted hat. "Oh, my gosh! I can't believe there is someone out here! I haven't seen a single soul in weeks! Wow, man!"

Feeling confused, Jake stuttered, "Um... I uh." The man didn't look like any member of the film crew. Maybe he was a contestant, and he got lost- he didn't look like anyone he met before the game began. The entire group came together for an intensive training session on filming, lighting, and engaging the audience to make the game captivating. It was a chaotic time and Jake knew it was possible to forget a face during all the commotion. One minute they were checking Jake's gear to make sure he only had items on the approved list. After that, they quickly learned how to work with cameras, and then they were forcefully shoved into boats and helicopters. Before

Jake knew what was happening, he was waving goodbye to the crew from the shoreline.

"Do you mind if I sit by your fire, my friend?" The man didn't wait for an answer as he seated himself on the ground next to the campfire.

Jake waved his hand. "Please."

"Thanks, man. I thought I was a goner for sure this time. I had a camp up there on the mountainside, but a bear ran me off. He caught a whiff of the rabbits I had been cooking. I hadn't had a meal in days, so I was really looking forward to it." The mans greedy eyes drifted over to Jake's boiling pot. "What's in the pot?"

A strange primal defense mechanism welled up in Jake's chest; he was hungry too. "Leftover fish skin, seaweed, and mushrooms. I've been sipping on the broth for a couple of days." Feeling like he was being tricked, Jake surveyed his surroundings for any hidden cameras. "Aren't you afraid you're going to get caught?"

Surprise crossed the man's face while he sarcastically laughed. "I doubt they will come here. There won't be any fuss about me. I'm no one, at least, not anymore."

Jake found the response to be weird. "Aren't you afraid you'll ruin it for yourself? I mean, don't you want to win?"

The man stared at Jake in disbelief, as if he had just heard the most absurd thing ever. "I ain't trying to win, diddly, mister. I'm trying to survive, just like you." Once again, the stranger's eyes wandered to the pot that was boiling. "Would you mind sharing a bit of that broth? I don't have anything to offer you as a trade, even though I'd like to. I have nothing to give you except for my company. Oh..." The man reached into his pocket and pulled out a harmonica. The light of the fire bounced off the scratched metal. Jake's mother would have referred to it as a well-loved instrument. "Never had much time to practice until that mess hit the fan, but I can play at least two songs all the way through."

"How did you get that in with no one seeing? Didn't they search your bag?"

The stranger looked confused. "No one saw me leave. I grabbed this on my way out." Looking Jake up and down with curiosity, he continued. "Are you okay, mister?"

Jake felt strange. Something was missing from the conversation. Either this man was crazy, or he thought he was the crazy one. "Other than being the hungriest I have ever been in my life; I'd say I am mentally sound."

The stranger appeared deep in thought, nodding his head as he considered his next questions. "What's your name, mister?"

"Jake and you?"

"Mike."

A silence passed between the two of them as they watched the fire for a minute. Deciding that the soup was heated enough, Jake used a t-shirt to grab his pot from the fire. After a few sips, he observed Mike, who had a hopeful look on his face. Jake didn't want to share, but his mother taught him better than that. He reluctantly passed the pot over to the newcomer. Mike selfishly drank the rest of the pot without considering giving Jake another sip. Jake felt a surge of anger flowing through him. He wanted to punch him in his greedy mouth. "Please, don't mind me. I didn't want anymore."

Mike's face reflected his shame as he realized what he had done. "Sorry, brother. I guess I turned into an animal."

Thinking about the countless days he had been hungry, Jake replied, "I guess this place will eventually make animals of us all."

"Indeed, sir." Mike glanced around the campsite. "I must say, your setup here is quite impressive. Any good food coming around? Bears, rabbits, etcetera? Hunting may not be my forte, but I have a knack for setting ruthless rabbit snares."

"I've heard a few bears in the area, but I haven't seen any rabbit tracks." Jake studied Mike; he was sure he hadn't seen him before; that much was becoming clear. Why was he here and how did he get on the island? "How did you get here?"

"What do you mean?"

Jake absentmindedly scratched his chin, which was now adorned with a new beard. The guy was either out of his mind or as dumb as a bag of hammers. "I mean, did you come by boat, or helicopter?"

"Oh, yeah. I took a boat."

Mike either meant he was brought by boat, or he stole a boat; Jake couldn't decide which. He figured he should focus on his line of questioning. "Have you heard from the producers or medics?"

Now Mike was really looking half crazy. "What are you talking about? What producers? What medics?"

Jake was convinced Mike meant he stole the boat now. "The producers; they were supposed to come by and refresh my camera batteries, but they never did. I haven't seen the medics either. I'm starting to worry. Have you seen them at all in the past few weeks?"

Mike looked around with a strange look on his face. "Am I on candid camera?"

It was Jake's turn to look at Mike with a crazy expression. "You *are* playing the game, aren't you?"

"Hey, man; are you crazy or something? Because if you are some kind of cannibal or backwoods weirdo, I'm not your guy." Mike rose from his seat and took a few steps back.

Jake mirrored Mike's actions and stood. "I'm talking about the game! You know, the game from the survival channel.

Where a group of ten contestants is dropped off in the middle of nowhere and whoever lasts the longest wins the money."

The realization of what Jake was saying finally registered with Mike. "Aw, man. You don't know, do you?"

The air around Jake felt cold and thin as he tried to remain calm. "Know what?"

"You think you're playing a game, huh?" Mike replied in a soft tone.

"Wait, what's going on? What are you talking about?" Jake's voice became more intense as panic crept in.

"Where are you from, brother?" Mike held up his hands to calm Jake.

"Oregon! I am here to play a game for a television show!"

In disbelief, Mike shook his head. "Dude, Oregon is gone, man. Hell, there is no United States anymore, or countries for that matter."

Jake grabbed his emergency walkie-talkie and pressed the big red button to call for help. The beeping began, its rhythmic tones echoing through the darkness. Mike was undoubtedly insane. Jake needed help ASAP! A hardened voice spoke from the speaker. "Who is this?"

"This is Jake. I have a situation here and..."

"Who is this, and how are you on this frequency?"

Mike wasted no time grabbing the walkie-talkie from Jake, forcefully hurling it down and mercilessly stomping on it. Someone called for Jake to respond until Mike stepped in with his foot for the twentieth time. "Are you crazy! They will find us!"

"That's the idea! And who are you calling crazy?"

With force, Mike gripped Jake's shoulders and yelled directly into his face. "It's gone! Gone! The world you knew is gone and those guys will hunt you down and kill you!"

"What are you talking about? Is my family in danger?" Jake's chest heaved with fear.

"What did you say your name was? Jake?" Jake felt like a scared toddler as he nodded. "Well, Jake, they are dead or prisoners by now if they didn't find a place to hide."

Jake's lungs burned as he tried to respond. Placing his hand against his shirt pocket, their picture served as a guardian for his sanity. "No, you're crazy!"

Mike gave Jake a gentle shake. "Jake, I need you to focus! We're already two months into World War Three. I'm not sure where or how it started, but one minute everything was okay in the world when I went to bed, the next minute I woke up to bombs going off in the sky and air raid sirens started blaring. Almost instantly, panic spread through the streets, triggering looting, and ultimately leading to the implementation of martial law. It didn't take long before the television started playing a message on a loop instructing us to stay in our homes until they rounded us up. That was all I needed to hear. I grabbed what I could and took off. I hid by day, moved by night. This is how I arrived here - by stealing a boat packed with fuel."

"That's impossible," Jake whispered. "How did I not see or hear anything?"

Mike looked up at the canopy of trees Jake had found to build his campsite. "It's possible that the trees prevented you from seeing or hearing properly, causing you to mistake the noise for animals or a thunderstorm. You might have noticed something if you had camped by the shoreline. We often overlook the bigger things when we're too focused on what's in front of us. Besides, I think Canada is trying to stay neutral for now. I don't see it staying that way. Roughly a week ago, I noticed military tanks were being transported to their borders. I have a feeling that our safety won't be guaranteed here for much longer, and we will definitely hear the wars raging around us."

In a matter of minutes, Jake experienced a nightmarish scene playing out right before him. Regardless of the consequences, he had to attempt to locate his family, even if it resulted in his own death.

The real game of survival had just begun.

The Edge Of Dark

MANY BELIEVE THAT THE complexities and capacities of the human mind are impossible to fully grasp. The age-old nature versus nurture argument becomes obsolete when people are pushed beyond their breaking point. I was thirteen when Tommy walked into my mother Sandy, and I's lives. It was nineteen eighty-five. My mother had been a widow for six years since my father's fatal car accident. If he hadn't left us the Apple Orchard drive-in movie theater, my mom said we would have been homeless and broke. My mother sold the house, and we moved into a small trailer behind the movie screen. The cramped quarters of the tiny trailer didn't bother me because we had a beautiful apple tree orchard in our backyard.

Despite the overgrown state of the apple orchard, big, beautiful red apples still grew. My mother welcomed any-one in need to take as many apples as they wanted to feed their families. The families who came for apples exchanged a service for my mother's generosity. They knew she was a widow, and that we didn't have a man to tend to the grass and repairs. On weekends, my mother and I would sit on a donated picnic table, enjoying the sight of the town's men mowing and weed-eating the grass. Occasionally, the men would fix up the snack shack or they would make repairs on our trailer. Every time the men left with their families and apple-filled baskets, they would tip their hats in a gesture of respect towards my mother. There was never any exchange of words. It was a mutual understanding.

The Apple Orchard drive-in theater was the lifeblood of our small community. Everyone knew each other in some small way. So, when Tommy Bass pulled into the drive-in, all eyes were on him. Tommy was handsome, that much was obvious. He bore a striking resemblance to James Dean, even in his style of dress. A pack of cigarettes was tucked into the sleeve of his white cotton t-shirt, and he wore dark blue denim jeans with rolled-up bottoms. Tommy combed his blond hair into a greasy pompadour style, resembling a nineteen-fifties dime store hood. With his confident stride, captivating conversation, and charming smile, he embodied the essence of prince charming. It would make the girls feel like jelly inside.

People tried their best to hide their curiosity as his red and white 1957 Chevy Bel Air coupe pulled up next to a speaker pole. His window went down, and that's when I got a clear view of him as he smiled at my mother and winked at me. I looked up at my mother and she had a strange look on her face, and her cheeks were flushed pink. Smiling, my mother tucked her ruby red hair behind her ear before returning to work at the concession stand. Before joining her at the stand, I cast one more glance at him over my shoulder. Tommy was watching us with that boyish grin on his lips. I can never forget the haunting effect of that smile.

Everyone in town was buzzing about my mother and Tommy's new relationship. People said they looked like a retro Ken and Barbie. My mother was the happiest I had ever seen her. Whenever Tommy was nearby, she laughed, smiled, and seemed to age ten years in reverse. We were all filled with pure joy. Sometimes it made me feel guilty. I missed my dad, and it felt like we were betraying his memory. According to my mother, our dad's wish was for us to be happy and enjoy life, and we did. That changed when Tommy moved in.

It was summer, school was out, and I was working full time at the concession stand. On weekends, we offered double features and unlimited popcorn refills. It was my favorite time of the summer because I got to stay up late; all my friends thought I had the coolest life. We were playing Teen Wolf and Weird Science the weekend Tommy moved in on us. Sitting on the car hood, Tommy had his arm around my mother as they watched the movies. Throughout the night, I noticed a growing pile of beer bottles near his car. When the movies finished and we cleaned up the snack shack and parking areas, my mom asked if Tommy could sleepover. She said he was too drunk to drive. I understood firsthand the anguish of losing someone in a car accident and how deeply it affected my mother and myself. There was no way I could bear to see that kind of pain etched on my mother's face again. My mother was my everything, and I'd go to any lengths to see her smile. Looking back on this moment, I realized it was emotional blackmail. Tommy spent the night and never left.

Each time I asked about Tommy leaving, my mother would come up with excuses for him to stay longer. It started with one night, extended to a week, and before I knew it, he had been living with us for six months. Eventually, I stopped asking my mother how long Tommy would stay and just accepted the fact he lived there. It didn't take long before the bruises showed up. The first one I noticed was on her wrist, as if someone grabbed her arm. The next bruise was on her cheek. I'd ask about it, but she said she was just clumsy or slept on her pillow wrong; it was always something. Before the year was up, Tommy didn't bother hiding who he was inside- he was the devil, I'm sure of it.

When the first sound of a can cracking open started in the evenings, silence filled the house; Tommy was the boss. We only left the house for school, to go to the grocery store, and to run the theater, and that was it. If we failed to be back home to meet his every demand, we faced the consequences. My mother's physical abuse became routine, and then he shifted his attention to me. I could tell he was gearing up to hit me when he balled up his fist and locked eyes with me after assaulting my mother. Tommy dared me to help her. I would wait for him to pass out on the couch before tending to her injuries. The abuse reached an unbearable level, resulting in the theater's closure and Tommy driving away families attempting to pick apples in the orchard.

My hatred for Tommy burned hotter than the fourth of July, but my mother loved him; I never understood why. Sometimes I felt angry at her because she allowed me to feel hopeless and powerless. I knew if I didn't do something, Tommy would kill my mother or me. Every night after Tommy would pass out and my mother cried herself to sleep, I snuck out of my bedroom window and ran as far into the orchard as I could go. The darkness provided me with a sense of safety and invisibility. No one knew I was there. I would lay flat on my back and gaze into the night sky. The stars twinkled, and the moon shone down on me like a blanket swaddling my broken heart. There in the orchard, I prayed, cried, and sometimes I would take off my jacket and scream into it. One night, I fell asleep in the orchard; Tommy was waiting for me on the front steps. It was the moment he had been waiting for. His face contorted into an evil mask as he balled up both of his fists. He jumped off the first step to the ground, and he began chasing me. I had no idea he could run so fast. Tommy closed in on me before I could escape.

I woke up coughing up the blood that had drained from my nose into my mouth; my head pounded, and my cheek throbbed. It had been morning when Tommy chased me. When I woke up, it was nighttime. Nobody came searching for me. Perhaps Tommy was hoping I wouldn't survive. He had been very vocal to everyone within earshot about his desire for me to leave.

I don't know how long I sat in the orchard before I came to my senses. A gentle breeze was blowing through the apple trees and a sweet fragrance filled my bruised nostrils. It was only when I faced death that I finally appreciated the beauty of the orchard. Row after row of apple trees stretched out as far as the eye could see. Now that it was summer again, the orchard was in full bloom. The synchronized dance of the lush green foliage was a mesmerizing sight as they swayed in the gentle breeze. With the wind tickling their stems, the ripe apples bounced on their branches, filling the air with their sweet aroma. It was at that moment that my mind snapped; rage filled every corner of my mind. Being surrounded by nature made me remember its dual nature of kindness and cruelty. Are we not akin to nature? If nature recognizes a toxic plant or animal species, does it not have a mechanism to eliminate it and start anew? That is how my brain ticked. There was no doubt in my mind that Tommy was toxic.

Once a week, I started walking to the library in town. It was the only place Tommy allowed me to go. He foolishly thought the library held no such thing as a threat. It made me feel good to know how dumb he was- most bullies are stupid. My research began slowly. I couldn't ask the librarian for help because I didn't want her to suspect what I was doing. I searched the card catalog for anything that may stand out. It wasn't until an old man named Sammy who spotted me one morning that I found what I was looking for. Sammy came to the library to buy the Saturday paper. Unlike the others who ignored my green and purple bruise on my cheek, Sammy threw fifty cents on the counter to the librarian and nodded towards my bruise. "Got yourself a whopper there, young lady."

I felt my neck turn red, but I responded without missing a beat. "Yeah, I wrecked on my bicycle. I guess I was riding too fast."

"I guess your mom has a runaway bike, too?" My heart raced as Sammy's intense gaze bore into my soul, leaving me feeling exposed and vulnerable. Embarrassment rushed through me. I had no response to his insult; I ran out of the library and into their meditation garden. I found a bench beside the water fountain and sat down. My eyes burned as I fought back the tears. With his paper tucked under his arm, Sammy took a seat next to me. "Sorry, kid. With age comes the tendency to speak before thinking, I suppose." After watching the fountain for a while, Sammy gave me his handkerchief. "Don't worry, kid. I didn't blow my nose on it." Sammy watched me with concern as I wiped my eyes and nose and sniffed back tears. "Forgive me for saying so, kid, but Tommy is a dirty old snake in the grass. I've seen his kind before, and you know how to deal with snakes? You take a garden shovel and break their necks."

With another swipe of the handkerchief, I turned to Sammy and said, "I'm too small. I've tried to find a way, but everything I find will take me away from my mother; she needs me."

Sammy nodded his head. "Let me tell you a story; what you do with it is up to you." I noticed a strange expression on Sammy's face when he locked eyes with me. As he started speaking, I felt a cold sensation travel down my spine. "When I was a little boy, my father was a drunk; he beat the stuffings out of me and my brothers with cane rods. Each night, my bedtime prayer was for God to take that man out of my life. The level of hatred I felt towards him was unparalleled. As the youngest in my family, I understand the sense of powerlessness you're experiencing right now. One day I was at school and the teacher had brought apples to class for all of us kids- we were poor, so having an apple was a real treat. The apples came from that very orchard you own today. Despite the initial backlash when your dad announced his intention to buy the land, he managed to win people over by building the theater in front of it instead of destroying the trees."

I knew the apple orchard was old, but I had no clue it was Sammy Clemens' old; he was eighty-five years old. "Wow, I didn't know that."

Sammy nodded his head and smiled. "Yep, it's been around for a while. Well, that day as we sat and ate our apples, one kid teased and said that if you swallowed apple seeds, you would die; talk about a kid-sized heated debate. The teacher came running out into the schoolyard and had it out with us youngsters. Upon learning the reason behind the commotion, she directed us to sit beneath the nearest shade tree and educated us about apple trees. One of the most interesting facts was about apple seeds."

"Apple seeds?" I asked, confused.

"Yep, if swallowed whole, you will just pass them in your next bowel movement, but if you crush enough of them... well, let's just say that your problem will go away."

"My problem will go away?"

Sammy eyed the bruise on my cheek again before he stood. "Yep." I didn't have time to ask more questions. He was in his pickup truck and pulling away from the curb before I could form a logical thought in my head.

Driven by a newfound mission, I stood up and made my way back to the library, eager to absorb every bit of information about apples and their seeds. Crushing enough apple seeds, as Sammy pointed out, can result in the production of natural cyanide. Did Sammy tell me to poison my mother's boyfriend? Sammy said his father was a drunk, and I wondered if his problem went away, too. It didn't take long for me to decide to make Tommy go away. Braving the blazing heat, I made my way home with a renewed sense of purpose. With every heartbeat thumping in my chest, I felt the power to kill Tommy coursing through my veins.

According to my mother, there is a place deep within each of us. She called it the edge of dark. I stood on that edge... I did what I had to do.

The day Tommy left; I discovered a hidden side of myself. I can't turn it off.

The Door

THE DREAM HE HAD was the same as before, one of many dreams like it. Over the roof of Henry's childhood home, a door hung in the air. The day was perfect, just like always, and as usual, Henry was twelve years old. He could feel the baseball glove hanging limp on his hand at his side. Squinting, Henry used his ungloved hand to shield his eyes as he examined the door more carefully. If he were to compare it to other doors that didn't hang in the sky, there was nothing too remarkable about it. It was a beat-up brown door with a dirty square window in the center. It hung there with no support, as if someone was about to open it. Henry could feel his heart racing. He knew what was coming; it always came at the end of the dream. It began with soft murmurs, but as if on cue, the volume increased, and the whispers grew louder. Next, the door began to open. It never opened all the way for Henry to see inside, but open enough to hear the blood-curdling scream of a man yelling, "Stay away, Henry!"

Henry shot up in bed, wide awake. The cold sweat clinging to his body made his pajamas feel sticky, while his heart pounded in an irregular rhythm. As his eyes opened, the room took on a distorted appearance, like peering through a dark, hazy tunnel. The door's lingering presence and the dread it harbored weighed heavily on his chest. The morning light rushed forward to bathe his fears with relief. Henry's bedroom came into focus. The curtains were drawn aside, and the windows were wide open. He could feel a gentle breeze blowing across his face as the birds chirped their morning sonnets. Henry exhaled and hoisted himself into a seated position.

Ginny watched Henry closely, her cup firmly gripped in both hands. This was nothing new to her. Since his father vanished without a trace, Henry had been suffering from nightmares for the past three years. She didn't even have the energy to summon up a look of concern on her face. The dreams had become such a routine, she could set her watch to them. Henry looked at her with a sweaty grin. "This is getting old."

Ginny nodded in agreement. "I'd say they are." With a deep sigh, she pressed on. "I understand if it seems like I'm nagging, but you need to consult a doctor or psychologist. It's gone on for way too long."

"I don't understand how a doctor or psychologist could be beneficial to me," Henry admitted. "I believe these dreams have significance, and I don't want anyone to convince me otherwise."

Placing her coffee cup on the nightstand, Ginny reached out and rested her hand on Henry's shoulder. "We can't keep living like this. *I* can't keep living like this; it's becoming too much, Henry. Your father has been missing for three years now. It's time to come to terms with the reality that he won't be coming back home. You said it yourself, in the dream, a man says to stay away. What if your dad's message is meant to be a warning? Surely that too could mean something?"

"I suppose." Henry hated to admit it, but that portion of the dream terrified him. "But the voice doesn't sound like my dad's. It sounds like something trying to sound like him, but the tone of voice is off. I can't explain it."

Ginny could see she was getting nowhere with the conversation. She never could. "I think I should move into the spare bedroom," she said as her voice shook.

"No, Ginny; we've never slept apart," Henry croaked as he fought back tears. He knew this was his fault, but he had no clue how to fix it.

"Since the dreams started, Henry, I haven't had a good night's sleep. I feel drained all the time. My boss gave me this week as a break from all the madness. I'm afraid he will fire me if things don't improve. I don't want to move out of our room, but I have worked too hard for this promotion at work. I waited until Jesse went to college to pursue a career and Mr. Thompson took a chance on me. I don't want him to think that hiring a stay-at-home mom was a mistake. Henry, I love having somewhere to go every day. My job is on the line if I don't get some sleep." Biting her lip, Ginny watched Henry to see how he would react. It became clear to him that she had been bottling up her emotions for a considerable amount of time. She spoke in a hurry, as if she had been waiting for the right moment to express her feelings, and now it had arrived.

Henry nodded his head as he considered her words. "I get it. I don't like it, but I get it. I know this is because of me and you're right. This has been going on too long." Henry thought long and hard before he said his next thought. "I think I can fix this, but I am going to need your support."

In a display of frustration, Ginny rolled her eyes and let out a sigh. "Henry... no, I..."

Henry held up his hand. "Please, give me a moment to explain. This door has been haunting my dreams for three years. I have written down every location I have seen them in. What if they are clues to find my dad?"

"You can't be serious. Henry, dreams hold no meaning. They are a reflection of your desire to find your dad. Even the

police stopped searching last year. Listen..." Ginny grabbed
Henry's hand. "Your dad is gone, Henry. He was a strange man,
and he too chased crazy dreams and look where that got him.
He followed one too many, and he vanished. Now, you want
to do the same thing. How am I to support this? Have you ever
thought about what would happen if you vanished as well?
Has it slipped your mind that they never discovered a body
or any sign of what happened to him?"

Henry knew she was right, but he couldn't stop the feeling
inside. The dreams were trying to tell him something and he
couldn't ignore it anymore. "It hasn't slipped my mind and I
know this hurts you." Henry roughly ran his fingers through
his hair. "I have to do this or not knowing will make me go
crazy - hell, it already has. Picture how it would be if it were
your dad, mom, or Jesse. Would you give up so easy then?"
The mention of Jesse's name caused Ginny's breath to catch.
She was their only child; it was a low blow, even for Henry.

Averting her gaze, Ginny examined her hand that was still
intertwined with Henry's before letting go. "Fine, you want
this? Then go. I can't stop you, but don't look for my support.
I've done everything within my power."

With a burst of anger, Ginny yanked off the sheets,
snatched her pillow, and stormed out of the bedroom, slamming the door. It wasn't in Ginny's nature to show anger in
this way. It was a clear sign Henry had pushed her beyond her
limits. People knew Ginny for her gentle nature, yet she, too,
had her limits. Henry hoped he could repair the damage when
he returned.

The vacant house amplified the sound of Henry's suitcase
zipper, reverberating in the void Ginny had left behind. She
had slept in the spare bedroom and left without saying goodbye. Henry left with a heavy heart after leaving a note on the
bed to tell her he loved her and that he would be back soon.

The summer heat made the drive to West Virginia brutal, but it was the last place his father had been seen. It was ninety degrees, and it was only seven in the morning when Henry woke up in his hotel room. The room was cheap, to say the least. The room had a strong odor of cigarettes and the carpet left black marks on Henry's socks after just a few laps. If the dreams didn't wake him up every few hours, some woman in the next room talking on her phone would have done the job. Henry felt well acquainted with the woman next door and her aunt Sadie from Georgia she gossiped about. However, the room was the least of his concerns. Henry wasn't there to sleep- not that he could anyway, with the car doors slamming and the telephone chit-chat next door. He was there to look for his father, or maybe the doors. He didn't know which.

The last person to see his father alive was his old friend Thomas. He lived in a back holler called Freeze Fork and the driveway to his cabin was murder on his eco-friendly SUV. Henry bumped and bounced up the mud and gravel path. It had been years since Henry had been home to Frozen Fork. The community may have been poor, but they were rich in love and family, and they had perfected what today's kids would call struggle meals. Henry had wonderful memories of sitting in his father's garden with a saltshaker and making a watery meal of tomatoes. His father couldn't muster any anger towards him. Seeing a 10-year-old boy with a saltshaker in one hand and a half-eaten tomato in the other, and juice and seeds running down his chin struck him as funny. All he said to Henry was, "Son, make sure you don't spoil your supper." Turning into Thomas' driveway, Henry couldn't help but smile to himself.

Whittling on a thick stick, Thomas sat on the porch in his rocking chair. He made no effort to acknowledge Henry's arrival with a wave or nod. That could only mean two things in the holler. Either they were expecting you or you were not welcome. You never wanted to meet a combination of the two. Henry didn't have a choice in the matter. He needed to speak with Thomas and that was that, or so he hoped. The sun illuminated Thomas' knife as he skillfully slid it across the wood. The ease with which the knife moved through the wood let Henry know the knife could slice through a tin can like a hot knife through butter. There were no dull knives in the holler.

As soon as Henry climbed out of his air-conditioned SUV, the West Virginia inferno greeted him. The temperature had risen to at least one hundred by the feel of it. Nervously, Henry shuffled his feet as he approached Thomas' front steps and coughed to get his attention.

Mid-swipe, Thomas's knife came to a stop as he scrutinized Henry above his spectacles. Henry couldn't help but notice how Thomas looked like a backwoods wizard. His white hair spread wildly in every direction, and it blended in seamlessly with his white beard. The only thing you could see on his face was his large, crooked nose and his sharp blue eyes peering out from under his round gold-rimmed glasses. "You sure took your sweet time."

"Sir?" Henry asked, confused.

Thomas resumed whittling once more. "You took three years to come and ask about your daddy." For the second time, he halted his carving and focused his eyes on Henry. "Well, isn't that why you're here?"

Henry felt stupid as he answered. "Yes, sir."

"Don't just sit there with your mouth open, you'll attract flies." Thomas pointed to a rocking chair next to his. Henry quickly climbed the front steps, waded through the pile of wood shavings, and took a seat as he was instructed. "So, do you know how to talk, or did your daddy hold back the fact that you're a simpleton? Surely you know more words than sir and yes, sir."

Thomas's directness caught Henry off guard after almost twenty years of not seeing each other, causing him to stumble over his words. "Um... yes sir... I mean..." Henry took a deep breath to collect himself. "I mean, yes, I can say more than yes, sir, and I am no simpleton."

"Neither was your daddy." Thomas studied Henry once more. "I see the same look in your eyes as I saw in his. I'm willing to bet that you're also a stupid fool. Bet you're up here chasing one of those crazy theories of his, ain't ya?"

"Sort of, yes. Most of all, I am looking for my dad. You were the last person to see him. Is there any information he shared with you that might help me find him?"

"No."

As the summer heat intensified, Henry fought to suppress his boiling anger and asked, "No?"

"Revealing what I know would lead to you chasing him, and that's not what Boot's would want."

It had been years since Henry had heard someone use his father's nickname. The sound of it made him want to fall to the ground and cry. "Thomas, if you know something, you have to tell me."

"I'm guessing you're having those dreams, right?" Without Henry giving him an answer, Thomas nodded his head with understanding. "Yeah, you are- I can tell. You have too much luggage under your eyes to lie to me about it."

"You know about the dreams?"

"Of course I do. Me and Boots were like this." Thomas's arthritic fingers twisted together. "We were like brothers. You never saw one without the other until he followed you to that newfangled city in Tennessee. Out of the blue, he came here one day, looking half-crazy like you do now, and started asking about the doors of Yonder Wood."

"The doors of Yonder Wood? What is that?"

Thomas flashed a warning smile at Henry. "It is a place we're not meant to go until we pass over to the other side." Thomas's knife ran across the wood once more. "My momma, rest her sweet soul, used to tell me stories about Yonder Wood. I made the mistake of telling Boots to scare him a little when we went frogging with my daddy. That night, we camped near the shooting range by the pond down there. Boots said I couldn't scare a ladybug, so I got mad and thought I'd spook him with Yonder Wood. The big dummy didn't get scared. Instead, he developed an obsession."

"Thomas, tell me what you told him. I need to know what happened." Henry sounded desperate, and he knew it, but he couldn't stop himself from asking for information.

"You ain't going to stop until I tell you. Am I right?" Thomas could see a look on Henry's face that told him all he needed to know. "Promise me that if I tell you, you will go home and not pursue it further. Can you do that, or do I have to get serious with you?"

Henry watched as Thomas lay his knife on his leg as he watched Henry for any sign of lies. Taking care not to reveal his plan, he responded, "I'll head back home."

Thomas froze as he considered Henry's words. He wasn't one hundred percent sure if Henry was telling the truth or if his empty threat scared him enough. If Henry was anything like Boots, he knew he would do the opposite of his words. In the end, he decided to tell him. "There are mysteries in this world that are not meant for us to know or comprehend. Once you become familiar with them, you can't pretend they don't exist, and they'll realize you're aware of their presence. They may or may not bother you. It all depends on whether you try to find them or try to cross into their world. Yonder Wood is among the many gateways to other destinations. My family knew about it because my great- great- grandpappy accidentally approached a door standing alone in the woods with no house around it. Someone or something forgot to close the door. If it was an accident or on purpose, we never could figure it out."

"Did he go through it?" Henry asked, wide-eyed.

"No, and he never said what he saw, but he heard voices whispering that grew louder as he got closer to the door. He snuck a peek inside, and one look sent him screaming all the way home." Thomas looked nervous as he reached into his back pocket to retrieve a handkerchief. Wiping the sweat from his brow, he continued. "After that day, my grandpappy saw no peace and because he told the story to his family and they passed it down through the years, we too have seen no peace. Not to mention, we see *him*." Thomas looked toward the dense woods surrounding his house. Henry followed his gaze and nausea swept over him as he noticed a dark figure peeking around a tree trunk covered in moss. "I think Boots tried to approach him and paid the cost."

Beads of sweat formed on Henry's upper lip as he tightly gripped the arms of his rocking chair. He tried to speak, but his face felt numb. The dark silhouette appeared almost human, with its greenish-gold eyes darting unnaturally between Henry and Thomas. It was eavesdropping on the conversation to see where it was going. When Henry found his words, the green eyes focused on him and caused his words to stutter. "What in the world is that?"

"The guardian of Yonder Wood. It will watch you too, now that you know they exist." Thomas turned his heavy gaze onto Henry. "I beg you not to pursue this. You have that nice wife of yours and a daughter who you will pass the dreams onto if you vanish. Do you want to sentence them to the same fate? Let it go, Henry."

The strange green-eyed creature from Yonder Wood opened and closed its mouth like it wanted to speak but couldn't. It looked excited as it awaited a decision. Henry could sense the creature's desire to inflict harm and suffering, yet it was held back by the rules it lived by. Chills ran down Henry's spine as he contemplated the idea of being watched by this creature forever. Revealing the secret of Yonder Wood to Ginny or Jesse would subject them to a fate more terrible than death.

Henry went back home, but was that really the end? If the dreams persisted, he didn't know if he would have the courage to stay away.

Cryonic

AN INTENSE SHIVER PAINFULLY passed through Willa's body. Her teeth slammed together over and over as she tried to open her eyes. *"Is this what death feels like? Did I cross over? Maybe this is the rebirth,"* Willa thought to herself. Her mind raced with the possibilities of what she might see when she opened her eyes. The cancer that had ravaged her body in life would never hurt her again. As she entered paradise, the suffering she had endured would finally fade away from her memory.

Willa managed to open her eyes for a moment, but a bright light immediately made her close them again. Her shivering gradually faded away as a warm and comforting feeling traveled up her body, starting at her feet. Willa inhaled deeply, letting the feeling of relief consume her as she exhaled. Once again, she attempted to open her eyes. The same bright light overwhelmed her senses, but she resisted the temptation to shut her eyes. She blinked rapidly, her eyes watering as she struggled to bring her surroundings into focus. Bit by bit, a white room materialized. Willa blinked a few more times until the room became clear. With a stiff body and a foggy mind, she attempted to remember the names of each item in the room. *"It's a char, no, a cheer... wait... it's a chair. And what is that? I know this one, I do. It's a label, no, that's not it. I know what that is; It's a stable, no wait..."* Willa thought she would stare a hole into the familiar object if she didn't think of the name.

"Table," Willa blurted out. The sound of her voice startled her. It had a hoarse sound and crackled with each syllable.

"Now, now, Willa; it's going to be alright," said a soothing voice by her bedside. Willa threw a sharp glance at the strange woman sitting beside her. The woman was beyond beautiful; her eyes were an unusual color of blue, and her hair was a perfect shade of blonde. The woman sat with her hands folded in her lap, exuding an unnerving sense of tranquility. As she studied Willa, her gaze remained steady and patient. Noticing Willa's confusion, the woman spoke once more. "My name is Stella. I will be your caretaker until you no longer need my services."

"My caretaker? What is that?" Willa asked in a whispered tone. The burning sensation in her throat matched the throbbing in her head.

"A caretaker is a person or employee that is in charge of the care of a person or animal." Stella's smile gave Willa goosebumps.

"Am I in a hospital?"

"You are currently residing at the New Horizon's Institute."

Willa surveyed her surroundings. The only difference in her room, compared to other hospital rooms she had experienced, was the absence of a telephone and a television. Turning her attention back to Stella, Willa probed further. "I don't understand; what is the New Horizons Institute and why am I here? Am I dead? Isn't this heaven?"

"No, this isn't heaven," Stella replied.

A wave of dread washed over Willa as her heart pounded. "You mean, I'm in hell?"

"No, Willa. You are at the New Horizons Institute. You are alive."

Willa shook her head. "That's impossible; I died. Everyone gathered around me and said goodbye, and everything went dark. I have stage four uterine cancer. There was no chance for me to survive. I remember my last moments and the room going dark." Stella grabbed a nearby notepad from a table next to Willa's bed and touched it with her finger. The object had a flat appearance, resembling a piece of paper with a chrome finish on the back. While Stella took notes on what Willa had shared, her face was softly lit by a white glow. It was nineteen ninety-six; technology like that didn't exist. "What is that?"

Breaking her concentration, Stella glanced up and smiled. "It's the latest iPad." Stella continued her explanation when she realized Willa needed more information. "It is a new technology that eliminated our need for paper. Your generation never saw these types of advancements." Stella looked down at her screen and swiped her finger across, then up and down. "Your file states that you were diagnosed with uterine cancer in nineteen ninety-five, and after a year of chemotherapy, you were placed in hospice care."

"Yes, but... I still am not understanding what is going on."

After placing her iPad on the table, Stella turned to Willa with a peculiar expression that she intended to be friendly. "The New Horizons Institute is a place for the study of science. Your family cryogenically froze you in nineteen ninety-six. They hoped a cure for your cancer would be found someday. At a facility called Continued Life, they froze your remains. Continued Life had one hundred and eighty-seven bodies; fifty of those bodies were those of family pets. When our archeologist unearthed Continued Life, they found that only ten human bodies were still viable."

"Wait a minute," Willa interrupted, throwing up her hand to stop Stella from speaking. "I never gave my permission to my family to do something like that! I was ready to move on; it was my time!"

"We acknowledge that some of you may have reservations about being awakened, but we couldn't abandon you given that your machine was still functioning. In an impressive feat, Continued Life enabled the cryogenic containers to be self-sustaining during a power failure. As I mentioned previously, only ten containers survived."

Willa's lips shook with emotion. "How long was I frozen? What year is it?"

"The year is three thousand and one."

As Willa thought of her family, friends, and the world she used to know, the room started spinning. Her own family froze her. They believed they would have another chance to see her, but she was left to face the world alone. Willa could feel herself fading into unconsciousness.

With three months of physical therapy, Willa was back on her feet. The staff at New Horizons were kind to her and took care of all her needs with precision. Counseling was an essential component of her daily schedule. During the sessions, they would present her with brief video clips showcasing the evolution of the world and its transformation into the utopia it had become. However, there was a noticeable difference in the food's taste. Fruits and vegetables were the only options available to them, as they no longer relied on animal slaughter for food. In the new world, everyone regarded death equally for all living beings, emphasizing the necessity to protect and preserve all lives.

On the fourth month of her awakening, as they called it, Willa could finally go outside. Of course, Stella was by her side. Willa couldn't have been more excited; she needed fresh air. As she walked towards the entrance and exited through the doors, all eyes fixed on her. The rush of sunlight bathed her in glorious warmth. Shielding her eyes, Willa took in the view. She had never seen a more beautiful place in her life.

Every corner had trees bearing different fruits, while lush green grass stretched as far as the eye could see. Instead of streets, there were white stone paths guiding people in various directions. Willa turned to Stella. "Where are the cars?"

"We found it was too damaging to our environment to continue with cars. The last car was made in the year two thousand eight hundred. Walking had become more beneficial for our over-all health and mental wellbeing."

Willa couldn't help but think Stella sounded like a re-hearsed schoolteacher. "How do you travel to far off distances like out of state?"

"You can borrow a winged glider from our hover stations. In time, you too will learn how to fly if you wish to travel further than your area. First, we show you around, and then we assign you a living quarter over there." Stella pointed into the distance. A sparkling white city glistened in the direction she was pointing. The appearance was like the sparkling white glitter of newly fallen snow.

In every direction Willa looked, she only saw happy people. In her old life, people would search for kind faces when they were out in public and encountered only a handful of nice people. Here, everyone seemed peaceful, and none of them had the strain of worry etched across their faces. People casually walked and chatted, not rushing towards their intended destinations, with a few taking time to sit under trees and indulge in reading or music. The birds were chirping, dogs were playing with anyone who gave them attention, and they looked well fed and happy. "I can't believe how amazing this is. Just look at that sky. It's so blue. Are you sure this isn't some kind of hologram? It's too perfect to be real."

"Holograms are unnecessary. As you can see, we have almost achieved our goals of restoring the earth to its original state." Stella looked around with pride. "Now, we are all caretakers of this planet. Come, there is much more to see."

By the time Stella gave her a break, Willa's legs were trembling. The world resembled nothing of what it once was. Although it was undeniably beautiful, Willa had a nagging fear of eventually growing bored. What would she do then? The people of the new world didn't need television or entertainment of that kind. Despite having books, music, and occasional live performances, something still seemed lacking. Since there was no paper available, reading a newspaper or writing a letter was impossible. Everything had moved to an age of computers; Willa's teacher in high school told her it would happen, but she didn't believe it. Until she woke up in the future, it had been hard for her to imagine a world that relied on technology. Willa's grandpa used to say, "Technology will always fail you." Yet there they were, they made it happen, and they found a way to reset the world. They discovered the cure for diseases and successfully eliminated world hunger. All forms of currency ceased to exist, and people began working together on everything. Skin color or financial status did not divide people, and there were no debates about who was better. It was a breath of fresh air.

In the fifth month, Willa transitioned to her own living space. Compact yet fully equipped, it met all her needs. There was no such thing as luxury or having more than someone else; everyone had what they needed. One of her favorite things about the apartment was all the plants and windows. Willa found nourishment in the sunlight that streamed through the windows, and she made it a nightly ritual to sit and stargaze. The sky seemed bigger without all the intrusive streetlights and the headlights of the countless cars whizzing by at all hours of the night. Small solar lights lined the walking paths, but they weren't like streetlights. The solar lights looked like stars on the ground. In the distance Willa could see lights on in various apartment buildings and she tried to guess who the people were and what their lives must be like.

Now and then, Willa liked to take night strolls. It felt odd not to have any worry about being targeted by a psychotic killer. There was no crime in the new world. The man who lived in her apartment building was the only person who made her uncomfortable. He looked angry all the time, and he only came out at night. Among all the people in the new world, he seemed like the only one who could explode at any moment. Willa couldn't help but notice his hawk-like gaze, and he made no effort to disguise the fact he was watching her. The angry man stood at the end of the hallway in the apartment building and stared out the window. Willa made up her mind to confront him about it. Living in the apartment building with someone who made her uncomfortable was not an option for her.

He was standing in his usual spot at the end of the hallway, just like always. With his arms crossed and his feet apart, he displayed a defiant stance. Willa was on the verge of speaking, but he spoke before she had the chance. "You're one of the frozen." It was a statement, not a question.

"Yes."

The man nodded his head. "Yeah, me too. How long have you been awake?"

Willa felt disoriented by his line of questioning. She was ready to confront this person who had been watching her and now he turned the tables on her. "Five months."

Once again, the man nodded. "I've been awake for a year. I was one of the ten like you." The man turned around to face Willa. "Apparently, my wife made the choice to have me frozen. I should have died in twenty, twenty-five. I worked for the government, and I had a heart attack at my desk. From the way it felt, I knew I was a goner. I can't understand why she would do this to me."

Willa shook her head. "I don't know. My parents did the same thing to me. I died of cancer; well, I thought I died. You said you have been awake for a year?"

"Yeah, I was the first one to wake up. All the residents in this apartment building were frozen. Except the eight-year-old little girl, she lives in an apartment with one of those things." Once again, the man turned around and gazed out the window. "I'm Rick, by the way."

"I'm, Willa. What do you mean by those things?" Willa asked.

"They didn't tell you either; did they?"

"Tell me what?"

Rick turned around to face Willa. "When I worked for the government, they hired me as a hacker. In the past, I made a lot of money as a career criminal by hacking into the bank accounts of wealthy people. I made a dumb and greedy mistake, and they caught me. Instead of throwing me in prison, they offered me a job. I had a wife and two kids; I knew I had to take the job. Next thing I knew, I had a heart attack and ended up in this utopia hellhole."

"How can you call this a hellhole? This place is wonderful. The people are..."

"Perfect?" Rick interrupted. "And nothing about this throws out red flags for you?"

Willa moved towards the window; the same spot Rick had occupied before. She looked out into the visual perfection. "I have to admit, I miss my old life and the way the world was sometimes, but not to the point I would think this place has red flags."

Rick stood next to Willa and looked out into the new world. "It took some time, but I mastered the new technology and gained access to their database. Nothing here is what it seems. Before I had my heart attack, there were wars and rumors of wars. The world was beginning its fall from grace. Chemicals, toxic fumes, and other pollutants contaminated the food supplies. Healthy people became sick and smart people lost their minds. People were dropping dead left and right. We witnessed people transforming before our very eyes, with technology becoming a household and handheld staple." Rick turned to face Willa as he continued. "AI was rapidly integrating into our daily lives. At first, computers communicated with humans in a way that resembled real people, but then developers gave them robot bodies. Before anyone was paying attention, they had robot dogs and humanoids working for the military."

Confusion washed over Willa as she shook her head. "What are you saying?"

"Humans no longer exist. Those are AI's. AI advancements led to wars that resulted in the extinction of humanity, according to their records. The remaining humans perished from consuming poisoned food, encountering deranged survivors, and suffering from dehydration caused by contaminated water. They met their demise one by one, with only the robots remaining. In an unexpected twist, they discovered how to not only survive but also enhance themselves and rebuild the world. Their aim was to safeguard human history and derive knowledge from it, which led to their discovery of us."

"So, you're implying that everyone outside this building is a robot?" In disbelief, Willa shook her head. "There's no way that's possible. They look too real."

"Oh, it's possible. Think about the length of time we were frozen. Not only is this the biggest discovery in hundreds of years, but there's an even scarier aspect to it." While staring into the darkened sky, Rick absentmindedly rubbed the back of his neck.

"I don't know if I want to know any more of this; I'm scared." Willa's body began to shake uncontrollably.

A sarcastic chuckle broke free from Rick's lips. "You aren't scared yet. Allow me to inform you about their upcoming plans. Our role will be to serve as experimental subjects for increasing human production."

The sensation of blood draining from her body overwhelmed Willa as she whispered her response. "I don't understand why they would do such a thing to us."

"Because they aren't human! They don't have feelings or understand that what they are doing is wrong. Regardless of our objections, they do not consider it important if we are used as cattle for their curiosity. We are going to be bred like dogs until our bodies give out and then they will have the fun of reviving us over and over again. Interested in knowing the reason behind the delay in waking you up? They healed your uterus and harvested your eggs, just like they did with the other awakened women. Currently, a warehouse is being constructed where babies will be grown using artificial life support systems. It will be a human baby factory. The plan is to force the men into contributing to the new human race." Rick cleared the sweat off his brow with a swipe of his hand.

"If someone made me have babies without my consent, I would die," Willa cried.

"Good luck with that; I've tried to kill myself fifteen times; they revive me every time." Rick's laugh sounded insane as he added. "*You*, my friend, are scheduled to undergo artificial insemination so they can observe a live birth. Aren't you comprehending it yet? We're like rats trapped in a beautiful cage!"

Willa frantically scanned her surroundings for a possible exit. "We could run and hide or form a rebellion of some sort."

Rick's lips formed a broken smile. "Boy, you sure are innocent, fresh from the farm. Look more carefully, Willa. Every move we make is being watched and every word we say is being listened to by them. I'm currently locked out of their system, so I can't gather more information." Rick flashed a middle finger to a picture on the wall of the New Horizons building. With a gaze filled with despair, Rick looked at Willa. "Welcome to the new world."

Willa could feel panic beginning to take hold. She was trapped in a hellish new world, with no hope of escape.

The Highway

OLIVER SAT AT HIS father's desk. Since he was a child, it had been off-limits, but it was something he had always wanted to do. The study was the sacred zone that was reserved for his father and no one else, not even his mother, who passed away three years ago. Wearing his funeral attire, Oliver looked around his father's room in silence. Immediately after saying goodbye, he found himself in his father's study without knowing why. Maybe he was hoping his father's death was some kind of hoax and he would pop out of a closet or drive up with his best friend Harry from the bar and say, "Thought I was dead, eh?" His father loved a good joke; he pulled a few doozies in his day. Everyone would laugh and say things like, "Good one Jackie boy!" or "You got me again, Jack! I'll get you back someday!" No one ever seemed to get mad at him because it was just his way- it was a love language.

Looking around the study, Oliver's chest filled with grief. Bookshelves that extended from the floor to the ceiling covered the walls behind his massive wooden desk. Hanging on the wall in front of the desk were various artists' framed artwork and black and white photos of friends and family. Across the wooden floor, there was a Persian rug adorned with delicate blue flowers. His father took so much pride in the rug that he wouldn't even wear shoes in his office. The image of his father's shiny black dress shoes carefully positioned next to his office door stuck in Oliver's memory. Forgetting to remove his shoes before entering his father's study filled Oliver with guilt.

Wiping his eyes, Oliver repositioned his upholstered chair to face the picture window with the reading nook. In the driveway sat his father's emerald-green nineteen forty-eight Buick Super eight. His father had bought the car when he was eighteen years old in nineteen seventy-two and fought with it every day afterward. No one could talk him into selling it, but Oliver's mother talked him into a better family car after she became pregnant with Oliver in nineteen seventy-six. It was a nineteen sixty-nine Ford station wagon, but it served their growing family well until nineteen eighty-five, when it finally chugged its last on the Tennessee highway. When Jack showed up in the Buick to save Diana and their three kids, his grin was impossible to miss. "A Buick's way saves the day," he said with a sarcastic laugh. Oliver's father never purchased another car, much to his disappointment.

The back of his father's Buick was where Oliver spent most of his childhood. The backseat wasn't too bad for three kids to share when the station wagon was in the shop for one of its countless repairs or when Jack insisted on using it for the family vacation and, of course, when the wagon broke down for the last time. There was plenty of room for Oliver and his two brothers to sleep, wrestle, play road games, and get into heated arguments. Being in the backseat during the summer was the worst. In a car with no modern air conditioning, the plush seat coverings made for a sticky hot ride.

With its classic American sleek design, chrome accents, and distinctive grille, the car made Oliver's friends green with envy. They idolized Jack for driving the vintage car, while Oliver felt self-conscious being seen in it until he reached adulthood. Sometimes Jack would get a certain sparkle in his eye before going for a long ride by himself in his beloved Buick. Oliver would give everything he owned to see his father driving that car again.

As Oliver looked away from the window, one memory that kept replaying in his mind was of him peeking under the study door to spy on his father. It was disappointing to a small boy to only see his father writing in his journal. Oliver had envisioned him examining maps, akin to an explorer charting his next escapade, or engaged in covert phone discussions with fellow spies. All he did was write in his journals and plan his next lesson for the students he taught at the college. The secrecy the study demanded from the entire family was something Oliver could never understand. The door always remained locked, and there was a strict silence surrounding the guarded room. Oliver's family just went through life as if it were a normal thing in every family to have a room no one could enter.

As Oliver got ready to look through his father's desk, he took off his coat and loosened his tie. Though it wasn't his intention, he couldn't bring himself to face his wife and sons' grief, as his own sorrow was already too much. Seeking a way to shift his focus, he found comfort in rummaging through his father's desk. Oliver searched the drawer in front of him, beneath the desktop. Despite being slimmer than the adjacent drawers, it proved to be a convenient storage space for paper, writing utensils, and a set of keys. Oliver threaded his finger through the metal ring, causing the keys to slide down. He knew those keys all too well- a Buick emblem hung from the ring. Like a bolt of lightning, pain coursed through Oliver's chest. Jack had parked his Buick for the last time two years ago. He placed the keys in the safest place he knew.

Oliver put the keys in his pocket and carried on with his search. The only items found in the polished hardwood drawers were papers from students, bills, and letters from loved ones. The last drawer he came to had a lock on it. Oliver took the keys out of his pocket and tested the smallest one on the ring. It fit perfectly. As he returned the keys to his pocket and opened the drawer, excitement filled his senses. Resting at the bottom of the drawer was a journal, bound in brown leather. Oliver reached out a shaking hand and pulled out the keeper of his father's secrets. Upon opening the cover, he noticed the aroma of leather and aged paper. Greedily, Oliver's eyes roamed over the words written by his father.

The further Oliver read, the more his confusion grew. It read like a journal, but his father didn't say a word about his life, wife, kids, his job, and there was no mention of the family vacations they took. He chronicled his life in his journal as if he lived in a separate town. There were people Jack talked about in the book that Oliver had never heard his father talk about before. Jack's journal entries read like chapters from a fictional book about a town, where he starred as the main character and incorporated actual towns and locations.

Jack never expressed his desire to be an author or mentioned that he was working on a book. The journal contained pencil sketches of various places and people, such as a barber shop, a gas station, and a newly opened sandwich shop at a pharmacy. Every picture Jack created had an extra detail Oliver noticed. It was the date, 1948. Flipping ahead a few pages, Oliver could see it was more of the same thing. In the journal, it mentioned a meeting with Nashville's mayor, a person named Cummings Sr. Jack mentioned running into him at the gas station.

Oliver reached into his front pocket and pulled out his smart phone. He searched for the mayor of Nashville, Tennessee, in the search bar. After only finding the current mayor, Oliver put in the name Cummings Sr. with the mayor of

Nashville, Tennessee, and someone popped up. It was a man who had been mayor from 1938 to 1951- he died in 1968. Oliver looked up from his phone and spoke out loud. "How is that possible?"

Shaking his head in disbelief, Oliver closed the journal. Jack was a one-of-a-kind and beloved individual, but the journal didn't resemble the person Oliver knew. The journal's version of Jack was bursting with thrilling adventures. He fearlessly charged ahead, unafraid of the unknown. The truth was, Jack maintained a calm and collected demeanor, often smiling, and stayed out of the spotlight when it came to anything adventurous. Oliver could remember the family going on a picnic at the Percy Priest Lake. A large cliff served as the jumping point for everyone into the water below. Jack was the only one who didn't jump. Oliver thought his father was afraid to jump and even felt ashamed anytime he thought about that day. In his journal, Jack recounted a drag race he took part in against a man in a black Chevrolet Fleetmaster. Oliver couldn't imagine his father doing anything of the sort. He had heard of authors living vicariously through their work. Oliver figured this was no different.

Oliver was on the verge of leaving the journal behind, but he changed his mind and took the leather-bound book before leaving. He locked the door behind him. Stepping outside with his father's journal, Oliver felt a smile break through his grief for the first time in nearly a week. The weather was unusually warm for October and the sun's heat beat down on Oliver's shoulders. He walked over to his dad's car and delicately caressed it with his fingertips. The automotive industry didn't make them like that anymore. In the present day, the automotive industry designs automobiles with computerized elements that are intended to expire, forcing consumers to invest in a new vehicle every four to five years. With proper care, Jack's car could last a lifetime.

As Oliver looked at the Buick, inspiration came to him. In a way, they had never done before, his father's keys inside his pocket called to him. Oliver's grin widened as he pulled his father's keys out of his pocket. While Jack was alive, it was forbidden for anyone to lay a hand on the Buick. Jack borrowed a friend's car to teach Oliver how to drive; that's how committed he was to no one touching his car. The car belonged to Oliver now, and there was no one to stop him from driving it home.

Slipping the key into the lock, the door opened, and Oliver slid into the driver's seat. That old familiar rumbling sound roared in his ears as Oliver turned the key. With a few presses of the gas pedal, the thick smell of gasoline filled the car as the engine let out a growl.

It felt as if the Buick was getting to know its new owner. As Oliver pressed the clutch and shifted into reverse, he could feel the energy of life coursing through him. The Buick seemed as solid as a tank as it glided past Oliver's electric SUV, which his wife convinced him to buy. He hated that car, but he didn't want to argue with someone who wanted to save the planet. Deep down, Oliver preferred the noise, the smell of gas, and the left-over vibration he felt when the car came to a rest at its destination.

Oliver backed out into the road and shifted into first gear. With a sudden jolt, the Buick came to life and surged forward. It felt like a racecar that had retired too early as Oliver shifted the gears until he hit sixty miles an hour. He rolled his window down and turned on the radio as he placed his elbow on the windowsill. The wind was warm, but Oliver didn't mind; he could feel his father with him. As he rolled down the highway, Oliver's mind started to wander. Since his father died, it was as if Oliver's mind had total recall of every memory he had with Jack. Memories that hadn't crossed his mind in years resurfaced while he was driving. With each memory that resurfaced, his longing to hear his father's voice became more desperate. Once again, grief overcame him as he grasped the magnitude of his loss. The absence of his parents left Oliver feeling isolated and alone in the world. He had two brothers, but they lived out of state with their families. Oliver was the only one who stayed close to his parents. Despite having his own family, he experienced an indescribable loneliness. It felt like he had lost all connection to the world, with only material possessions left by his parents as a reminder of their presence.

A peculiar wave of nausea rolled through Oliver's stomach. It was unlike any sickness he had experienced before. Prickling pain twirled through his insides like a cactus and his vision became blurry. In an effort to regain his vision, Oliver blinked repeatedly and removed his foot from the gas pedal. Much to his surprise and terror, the car didn't slow down; it sped up. As the Buick sped towards its demise, Oliver could feel his back pressed against the seat, helpless as the car took control. In a state of bewilderment, Oliver clung to the wheel, fearing for his life. It was unnerving how the car never swerved or lost control. The sensation was as if someone else was driving, keeping a steady pace. The radio station that played all the top songs from the eighties suddenly switched to music from the forties, specifically "Twelfth Street Rag." Oliver was well-acquainted with the tune. Jack played the song so often that Oliver could hum the entire song without missing a beat.

The insane song playing on the radio became louder the faster the car went down the highway. Just when Oliver thought he would toss his cookies, the car slammed on its brakes, sending his chest into the steering wheel. The breath temporarily left his lungs as the engine rumbled under the hood. It sounded like a monster that was daring Oliver to try anything funny. Oliver pushed himself away from the wheel as his eyes focused and his ribs ached. What he saw was unreal. The four-lane highway had transformed into a dirt road. A small rural town was in the distance. Oliver's view was filled with the sight of antique cars from the 1920s, 30s, and 40s driving around, while men on horses added a touch of the Old West. As darkness fell, a young man lit the streetlamps along the roads in town.

Oliver felt like he had entered the Twilight Zone as he tried and succeeded in driving the car once more. He gently pushed the accelerator as he made his way into town. Upon finding a place to park on the street, he noticed the townspeople staring at him. After Oliver exited the car, his attention was drawn to a store on the other side of the road. The store he saw matched the drawing in his father's journal. Oliver walked across the street to the Save A Dime grocery store. A sign on the window advertised, "Experience the flavor of our just-picked corn! Two pounds for just five cents!"

"You can't beat our prices on farm fresh produce, sir." Oliver jumped and turned to face the voice behind him; it was the shopkeeper. He had on a dark blue suit with an apron hanging over it. He looked charming with his broom in hand and a smile on his face. "You must be new in town, but I could have sworn when you pulled up in that machine over there that you were someone else. Do you know him?"

"Know who?" Oliver asked, puzzled.

"Jack; he drove a car just like that. I haven't seen him in a while. He used to be a regular." Smiling, the man eagerly awaited Oliver's response.

Oliver buried his grief by swallowing the lump rising in his throat. It was the first time he had to tell someone the bad news. "Are you a friend of his?"

"Why, sure! He is one of our finest citizens."

"Citizen? You mean he lived here?"

Oliver caught a glimpse of the shopkeeper's smile weakening as he was being scrutinized. "Yes; is there something wrong young man?"

Oliver answered instead of asking questions, recognizing it wasn't the right time. "Yes, sir. I'm his son. I hate to be the bearer of bad news but my father, Jack, passed away unexpectedly last week. I was just taking his car for a drive and somehow ended up here."

The shopkeeper nodded his head somberly, and what remained of his smile vanished. "I had a feeling it was something like that when our weekly date at the Pharmacy lunch counter didn't happen for a few weeks. I'm going to feel his absence for sure. The best friend I've ever had." The shopkeeper shot Oliver an odd expression. "Why did he never mention you to me?"

"He never mentioned you to me, either."

"Well, isn't that a pickle?" The shopkeeper used his free hand to rub his chin. "I suppose you would like the key to his house?"

"Wait, he had a house?" Oliver asked in disbelief.

"Come on in and I'll fetch those keys for you. Oh, and by the way, I'm Cooper."

When Oliver was a child, his grandpa Silas would tell him stories about the past, including his experiences shopping at stores like Save A Dime. The grocery store was just as incredible as Silas had described. The store had shelves lining each wall, stocked with canned goods, hair products, medicines, perfumes, sewing kits, and more. In front of one of the shelved walls, there was a counter where you could buy meat and cheese that could be sliced and weighed for your convenience. Standing shelves at the center of the small store showcased sugar, spices, and more canned goods. Wooden barrels, filled with vegetables and fruits, including a single barrel of white saltine crackers, were strategically positioned throughout the store. The sights and aromas around Oliver caused his stomach to rumble. *"None of this could be real,"* Oliver thought to himself. He reached out and grabbed a saltine cracker- it felt real. Lifting it to his nose, Oliver smelled the cracker before placing it in his mouth- it tasted real. The cracker had a combination of saltiness, crunchiness, and a delicate buttery flavor.

When Oliver lifted his eyes from the cracker barrel, he spotted Cooper watching him with a grin. "Best saltines in four counties! Try another!"

Oliver protested by waving his hand, feeling as guilty as a child caught with his hand in the cookie jar. "Oh, no. I'm so sorry. I just..." Oliver almost said, "I never saw crackers packaged like these." If he was alive, which at this point he didn't know, something crazy had happened in his father's car. Until he pieced it together, he had to remain nonchalant when encountering others. "I just never saw such tasty look-ing saltines."

Cooper agreed with a nod. "Oh yes, they are the finest around. Here you are."

Oliver held out his hand and watched as Cooper dropped the key to his father's secret house. He had a nagging question, and he didn't think it would raise any suspicion. "Why do you have the key to his house?"

"Jack said he was always losing keys, so he left it with me. He'd pick it up when he was in town." Cooper scratched his head. "He never would tell me what he did for a living. He said his job is why he was gone a lot. What did your father do for a living?"

Thinking fast, Oliver blurted out the first thing he could think of. "He oversaw a couple of railroad projects. I don't know all the details about it, but it kept him busy." Oliver could see his answer was satisfactory, so he moved on. "Can you tell me how to get there? He never brought me out this far."

"Sure." Cooper walked outside onto the sidewalk. He pointed down the road. "Keep going on this road until you spot a large red barn. Make a left turn and keep going in that direction for at least a mile. You'll come across a little yellow house in the field. There's a large windmill behind it."

Before getting back into his father's Buick, Oliver shook Cooper's hand. He diligently followed the directions and discovered the small yellow house in the midst of a field, exactly as Cooper had described. Oliver felt conflicted about his father's mysterious double life in the strange town. After stepping out of the car, Oliver headed towards the front door. He placed the key into the lock and let himself in.

The house had a musty, old smell, and only the living room had any furniture—a writing table, a chair, and an oil lamp. On the table sat yet another leather-bound journal, waiting to be claimed by its owner. Oliver seized a pack of matches that was placed beside the lamp. Striking a match, he lit the lantern and took a seat. With the cover opened, Oliver began reading his father's words.

> *"Oliver, I have a feeling it was you who un-*
> *covered my not-so-little secret. I know you are*
> *confused. When I first traveled back in time by*
> *accident, I was confused. Not long after buying*
> *the Buick, I gained the ability to time travel.*
> *It first occurred when I was eighteen, and I*
> *noticed it happening every time my mind was*

not focused while driving. After reaching adulthood, I stumbled upon a study regarding highway hypnosis. When drivers are lost in thought, their minds switch to autopilot mode. For some reason, my thoughts transported me to 1948. At first, I thought I was dreaming, or maybe I had died, but after a while, I realized it was all real. I found myself unable to stay away. I have the freedom to be whoever I want to be in this place. In my time, however, I am a family man, a college professor and a mild-mannered man. Being here allows me to experience a life full of adventure. Every time I return, it's always 1948. They never notice how I'm getting older with each passing year. Life has been nothing short of amazing for me. Though both of my lives have been fantastic, Oliver, you cannot stay in this place. This situation has divided me, and I am filled with shame. It's time for you to go home and live your life alongside your family. This place is stuck in time and will never change. If you aren't careful, you will get stuck here with them; don't lose yourself. I love you, son. Go home. Just get back in the Buick and think about home."

Knowing the truth about his father and this town frozen in time left Oliver with a strange feeling. Maybe it was real, maybe it wasn't. All he knew was that he wanted to go home-he couldn't promise he wouldn't return.

One Last Beer

IT WAS A HUMID New York summer night and, once again, Charlie couldn't sleep. It was no secret that he hated the summer months; he let everyone know fall was his preferred time in the Big Apple. The fall season in New York offered a refreshing breeze and a vibrant nightlife. During the summer months, however, the people experienced sweltering heat, irritability, and opted to stay indoors until the sun mercifully disappeared below the city's horizon. By July, Charlie began experiencing the onset of seasonal depression. Nighttime offered him a much-needed respite from the summer blues. Nighttime strolls in New York surpassed daytime walks. Despite the sticky humidity clinging to his skin from the heat released by the sidewalk, Charlie still found pleasure in the city's sights and smells. The aroma of the exhaust from the cars passing by, mixed with the smell of food from various restaurants and food carts, made it feel like home. Along with the smells of food cooking, there was a pleasant scent of flowers and leaves, heated by the sun, drifting through the air from the nearby parks.

The summer nights brought the streets to life with various activities. As Charlie made his way past bars, open windows, rooftop parties, and restaurants, he was surrounded by the sound of people talking, laughing, and music. The atmosphere in New York at night was invigorating, as if any dream could become a reality. Charlie loved how the streetlamps sparkled like diamonds against the night sky as he walked the streets. The stars couldn't be seen too clearly in New York, but the streetlights were close to the same thing. Charlie was a loner, but he never truly felt alone in the city that never sleeps. Where else could you get your daily dose of mingling with people without interacting with anyone in any other place other than New York?

There was nowhere else Charlie would rather be than the Dirty Dawg. The Dirty Dawg was the best dive bar in town. Most people like fancy bars with their pounding music, fancy drinks with umbrellas and fruit, but not Charlie. At The Dirty Dawg, you could enjoy the best cold beer on tap and tasty, budget-friendly mixed drinks. A gentle and inviting warmth enveloped the room, inviting people to stay.

Red neon lights displayed the words "Dirty Dawg" and blinked as if they were on the verge of burning out. Charlie suspected the neon was past its prime, yet the lights remained resilient until they decided it was time to fade away. The outside of the building had become weathered, and the door had worn-out from forty years of patrons passing in and out. The front windows were grimy, yet a comforting light remained visible. Just like on previous sleepless nights, Charlie walked through the door. With its dim lighting, the bar's atmosphere was filled with shadows that extended over the rustic wooden tables and mismatched chairs, as well as the individuals seated there. The fragrance of stale beer, greasy food from the kitchen, and cigarettes of long past filled the air. Charlie headed towards the barstool at the end of a wooden bar that resembled a repurposed relic from an old ship. The surface, although marked with scratches and stains, remained impeccably shiny.

The bartender, towering at six foot four, was a Vietnam veteran. Despite his rugged appearance and tattoos, he always spoke with kindness and never revealed the horrors he had witnessed. Over his clean white T-shirt and blue jeans, Frank wore an apron with stains. As he wiped a glass with a dingy colored towel, he always greeted Charlie with a friendly nod upon entering the bar. Charlie was sure he did that for everyone who came to visit, but he liked to pretend Frank did it because he saw Charlie as a friend. Charlie raised his finger to signal Frank, even though the bartender was already paying attention to him, he did it out of habit. Frank moved closer to Charlie and strained to hear his order over the loud music. "I'll take an Irish whiskey shot and a draft beer, please."

With a nod, Frank got busy with his tasks. Charlie, who despised making eye contact, couldn't resist stealing a quick glance around the bar while waiting for his drinks. An elderly man, hunched over his glass of beer, was trying to explain the history of the Dirty Dawg to a tired-looking patron at the bar. The weary man, showing no interest, appeared indifferent, yet the old man continued speaking as if he were oblivious. In the corner of the cozy bar, a bunch of bikers sat, enjoying beer, and shared boisterous laughter over their own jokes and anecdotes. Every so often, one of them would stand up and select another popular tune on the jukebox. The bar's mix of grit and warmth captivated Charlie. Amidst New York's ever-changing landscape, the Dirty Dawg provided a sense of stability and comfort. You could rely on this dirty haven if you wanted an escape from the fast pace and chaos of the city- at least, that's what Charlie believed until this night.

Charlie was on his third Irish whiskey when the door burst wide open. Every voice hushed, except for Creedence Clearwater Revival, singing loudly from the jukebox. All eyes were on the door as the stranger yelled, "This is a stickup!"

Charlie sat frozen on his stool, gripped by fear at the sound of
"Nobody moves, nobody gets hurt!" The pleasant buzz he had
been experiencing vanished like a burned-out lightbulb. After
three hours of non-stop talking, the old man finally fell silent,
much to the relief of the weary guy. The bikers positioned in
the corner stood and faced the robber. The action wasn't lost
on him. Concealed beneath his coat, the robber redirected
the shotgun towards the back of the room. "Don't get brave
boys and you'll live to see tomorrow."

A biker with a thick brown goatee and tattoos on his bald
head had sharp blue eyes that could kill. "If I live, you won't."

Charlie risked a closer look at the robber. He wore a hooded trench coat with a neon green mask that covered his mouth
and nose. Underneath the coat, the robber aimed the shotgun
squarely at the biker. "A death wish; I like it. Now sit down or
I'll make your friends head into a canoe." Against his will, the
biker reluctantly settled into his chair and gave a menacing
look. "Good, boy. Now, make sure your little bicycle friends
do the same." The robber shifted his focus to the bartender.
"You, there. Empty the cash register into a bag and be quick."

Frank shook his head. "You don't need a bag for what I
have in the till. I only have about eighty bucks."

"Don't lie to me, man!" The robber yelled.

From the register, Frank withdrew three twenty-dollar
bills and two ten-dollar bills. "This is all I got, partner. We take
credit cards these days, or don't you know that?"

Charlie sensed the robber's panic as he took the cash from
the bar, placed there by Frank. Following that, the intruder
jammed the gun into Charlie's face. "You! Your wallet! Now!"
Hands shaking, Charlie did as he was told and threw his wallet
on the bar. Taking the credit cards and cash, the thief flung
the wallet down onto the floor. Going around the room, he
gathered small amounts of cash and credit cards, one after

another. Charlie wanted the biker with the goatee to be the breakthrough hero, but he begrudgingly went along with it.

The haggard man sitting next to the old-timer caught the robber's attention. The man seemed ignorant of the fact that a robbery was happening, unlike the other people in the bar. He casually drank his beer while all hell was breaking loose around him. With quickened steps, the criminal approached the weary man and firmly placed the gun against his back. "I don't think you heard me, mister. Your wallet or your life!"

The tired man set his unfinished beer on the bar and casually retrieved a pack of cigarettes from his shirt pocket, lighting one up. Nervously rocking back and forth, the robber's impatience intensified. Charlie had never seen a murder before and thought this night was going to burst his protected bubble. The man's weary voice remained calm, yet carried a sharp tone as he addressed the thief. For an unknown reason, Charlie felt more frightened by the tone of his voice than the gun-wielding robber. It wasn't what he said, but how he said it. "I have five dollars left in my wallet and I'm going to buy one last beer with it." The worn-out man took a puff from his cigarette and shook his head in disbelief. "You don't know me, so I'm going to give you some sound advice. You don't want to know me."

The haggard man's sideways glance at the robber filled Charlie with a fear he had never known, sending hot and cold chills throughout his body. Charlie had only seen that look in dogs who were about to attack, except this man's eyes were tinted red. He could tell that the robber saw the look too and decided to turn and run out of the bar. Everyone watched in silence as the haggard man drained the contents of his beer, crushed out his cigarette, and pulled out his wallet. He placed a one-hundred-dollar bill on the bar as he stood and said, "I think I'll pass on that last beer." Despite the dim lighting,

Charlie could clearly see that the man's wallet was brimming with cash. He left the bar without saying anything else, giving Frank a nod.

Once the police arrived, took reports, and a news crew appeared, Charlie spoke to the police and then left. He had no intention of being part of the evening news segment. He walked with his head down all the way to his apartment, ignoring the joyous voices of those who didn't just get robbed. Once Charlie slammed the door shut, he made sure to lock every lock on it. His body was sore from the muscles that had locked up with fear. With every joint in agony, he fell onto his bed and passed out.

The following day, Charlie woke up at noon, which was unusual for him as he had never slept past eight am before. A throbbing head and achy muscles were constant reminders of the tense night that passed. Charlie's cellphone blinked with unanswered messages. There's no question that a few of the calls came from his mother- she would phone him a minimum of ten times every day. He picked up the phone, pressed the voicemail button, and endured his mother's long-winded discussion about his father's health troubles. The last message captured Charlie's attention. "Charlie, baby, it's mom. Have you seen the news this morning? That bar you like got robbed last night. I hope you weren't there when it happened. Please call me. Some kind of shootout happened. Please call me."

Charlie felt confused as he crawled out of bed and headed for the living room; there wasn't a shootout. Grabbing the remote, Charlie tuned into the local news. The big news of the day revolved around the Dirty Dawg. Without the gentle red neon glow, the dive bar seemed barren and neglected when viewed in the daylight. The reporter, with her fire-red hair and matching lipstick, delivered her words dramatically as she covered the dive bar tragedy. "Lisa Brenna here, reporting live from outside the Dirty Dawg bar on main street for New York This Morning. Behind me, you can see the bar is dark and quiet, which wasn't the story last night. I spoke with someone who was there when the night of terror began." The screen transitioned to a previously recorded clip. It was the old man that liked to ramble. "Mr. Donahue, can you please give me a rundown of what occurred at the Dirty Dawg last night?"

The old man cleared his throat and tried to look serious as he recounted his story. The people out there in TV land just became the biggest audience he had ever had. "Last night, a man wearing a hooded trench coat and a bright green face mask stormed in with a shotgun. He took every cent I had and then he robbed everyone else except for one guy; I think he was an angel or something."

After his last remark, the clip was abruptly cut off and when it returned to her, Lisa stood in front of the bar with a smirk on her face. "According to the police, they have found the suspected individual. Our airborne news team has captured footage of the incident." As Lisa Brenna narrated, a live video played showing what the cameras were capturing. Charlie activated the mute button. A body was floating on its back in the Harbor. The sight of the body, credit cards, and money moving in rhythm with the waves gave Charlie goosebumps on his arms. He could recognize the bar robber, despite the face being blurred and the green mask covered in blood spatter. It was the scum that took his money; Charlie knew it had to be. Repeatedly, the news anchor questioned the identity of the person responsible for his murder.

It was the haggard man with the devilish side-eyed glance, and Charlie knew it. Something deep inside told Charlie this man was dangerous. The old man was wrong. He was no angel. He must've gone after the robber and killed him. Did the robber push the buttons of a serial killer or was he a vigilantly that was sick of people getting away with taking from others? Could it be possible that he was something entirely different, and the robber beckoned death to his front door?

Charlie made the choice to quit drinking at bars. From time to time, Charlie was convinced that he spotted the man who haunted his dreams on the streets of New York. He disappeared when Charlie took a second glance. Charlie couldn't shake the feeling that it wasn't over.

After Midnight

"YOU'RE LISTENING TO KMB Utah radio, home of the classic hits. I'm grateful that you're here with me at this late hour. Allow me to introduce myself. I'm Jackie Tone. Friday is almost here as we approach midnight. TGIF, am I right? We'll overcome this long week together, one classic hit at a time. Here's the Rolling Stone's with Gimmie Shelter."

Late at night, Ron enjoyed listening to the radio. Driving a semi-truck could get lonely if it weren't for the voice of Jackie Tone and her smooth hits to keep him company. Long haul truck driving wasn't for the weak. For an individual who cannot bear being alone, remaining silent for hours while driving would drive them insane. Ron enjoyed being alone, but his favorite thing was the nighttime view of the world. Utah was his favorite. The vast deserts of Utah created a whole new world at night, seemingly without any boundaries. From time to time, massive rock formations would emerge, or the distant lights of a town would illuminate the horizon. As night fell in the desert, the air grew cool and crisp, and the sky sparkled with an abundance of unobscured stars. The background noise of crackles and pops from his CB radio served as a reminder that he was never completely alone. There was always someone out there, driving alone on a dark road and wanting to talk.

Glancing at the clock on the radio, Ron bounced over the rugged highway. Ron drank his truck stop coffee, which had turned cold after hours of sitting in his cup untouched. He didn't know why he was drinking it in the first place- he felt awake. The moon was full and cast eerie shadows on the desert sand and across the road, giving the sense that something was in the air. The song on the radio started to fade in and out, while the CB crackled with static. As Ron adjusted the volume, a set of bright, round headlights flooded his side mirrors with a blinding light. He held up his hand to shield his eyes.

Ron risked a few glances in his side-view mirror and saw the semi-truck riding his bumper. He reached over and grabbed his CB. "Hey, bumper humper, can you back off? There is enough road for the two of us." Ron watched as the truck behind him fell back; his message was received loud and clear-or so he thought. Ron anxiously watched as the semi-truck increased its speed and swerved into the opposite lane. Despite being a no passing zone, Ron had seen this move a million times late at night - when there were fewer drivers on the road, some laws would be broken. When the semi-truck's headlights stopped blinding him, Ron made a chilling discovery. Ron squeezed the button on his CB again, trying his best to maintain composure. "Driver, your engine is on fire! I repeat, your engine is on fire! Do you copy?"

Ron watched in horror as the semi gained speed as it passed him. Flames engulfed both his engine and brakes. A mysterious blue-violet light filled the truck's cab, casting an eerie glow, and the height of the truck made it impossible for Ron to see the driver or determine if he was awake. Ron squeezed the CB button harder this time. "Driver, do you copy? You are on fire!"

The CB finally springs to life, catching Ron's attention. He anxiously awaited a response, his heart thumping in his ears. A strange, crackling laugh burst out of Ron's speakers. The voice was hoarse and scratchy. "It's all good in the neighborhood." The driver's elongation of the 'O' in the word neighborhood was unsettling. Ron could tell that the driver was a few cards short of a full deck, yet the whole scenario felt creepy. It felt like he had stepped into a strange alternate world. Ron knew about truckers who had encountered a type of cabin fever from being isolated on the road for long periods, but this felt different. It was haunting.

Goosebumps appeared on Ron's arms as he gave his response. "You're not comprehending the situation. Both your engine and tires are ablaze." Ron's voice echoed through the silence, "You have to pull over!" Receiving no response, he attempted to contact the driver once more. "Can you hear me? I'm telling you again, you're on fire!" Just as Ron finished speaking, the moon emerged from behind a cloud, illuminating the road ahead. The truck beside him was barreling towards a sharp curve, making a collision almost certain. "Sir, there's a curve right ahead! Slow down and pull over! I am equipped with a fire extinguisher! I can help put you out while we call for help!"

A psychotic laugh echoed from the speakers as the semi-truck accelerated past Ron. The sight of the truck's trailer swaying filled Ron with horror. He was sure the truck would tip over, but it recovered quickly. The semi-truck looked like a flaming chariot as it barreled down the highway like a speeding bullet. Ron could only see disaster happening as he tried one last time to reason with the lunatic. "Sir, you're going too fast. You are on fire and there is a dangerous curve coming towards you! Slow down! Can you hear me?"

The CB popped and crackled as the strange voice spoke for the last time. "I'm coooool as a cucumber, good buddy. Don't you worry your pretty little head about me."

With amazement, Ron watched as the semi-truck miraculously rounded the curve and vanished from sight. Ron's truck's dash lights blinked chaotically as he got closer to the curve. The radio's volume turned itself up and blasted, 'Don't fear the reaper'. No one would ever believe Ron if he told them of the insanity that was unfolding in front of his eyes. He wasn't sure if he would believe it if someone else was telling him this story over four a.m. coffee. Without a doubt, Ron knew he wasn't crazy, and his eyes weren't playing tricks on him. Something wild was happening- something unnatural. In his thirty-year trucking career, Ron had witnessed countless extraordinary sights, but this took the cake.

Slowing down, Ron took his time rounding the curve as sweat poured down his cheeks- there was no way he would have the same dumb luck as an unhinged truck driver. The jake brake growled and shook the inside of the cab as Ron gripped the steering wheel and turned as smoothly as he could. He could feel his tires bouncing under the strain of the intense curve, but he held on as he made it safe and sound.

Ron felt a wave of relief as the road came into view when he rounded the corner, and he saw that the semi-truck had vanished. In disbelief, Ron muttered to himself, "I can't believe it."

There were no cars in sight on the road ahead, giving Ron an unobstructed view of the expansive Utah desert for at least fifty miles. It defied all logic for the blazing truck to have traveled at such a speed. As soon as Ron saw the burn marks on the road, he slowed down to a crawl.

Ron stopped his semi-truck and stepped out, examining the road. The pavement was charred, and the road was hot to the touch. The scent of burned rubber, diesel fuel, and tar filled the air. His stomach churned as the cold coffee he had gulped down earlier fought like a caged monster fighting to escape. All that could be heard was the low, rhythmic rumble of his engine, the sound of his breath, and the distant chirping of night bugs.

Ron surveyed the area but couldn't identify any side roads in his line of sight. There was nothing but the desert. Like a phantom in the wind, the other semi-truck had disappeared. Maybe that was it. Was the lunatic a ghost or something more sinister, preying on isolated drivers along the empty roads?

The rest of Ron's drive was a complete blur. It all felt like a dream. It was five a.m. when Ron pulled into a truck stop café. After the night he had, a hot breakfast and a fresh cup of coffee were exactly what he needed. Only one customer was seated at the counter at the Cuppa Coffee. Ron liked it like that, so he could enjoy his meal in peace. Ron settled down a few seats apart from the elderly gentleman seated at the counter. A tired-looking waitress walked over and handed him a menu. "Care for some coffee, love?"

Ron returned her weary smile. "Sure, and I'll take the trucker sampler breakfast with biscuits."

"You got it." The waitress scribbled his order on a greasy notepad. With a wink, she took his order to the kitchen.

"Looks like you just came off Deadman's Highway."

Ron shot a look over at the old man, who was holding his coffee cup in the air as he awaited a response to his comment. In a confused tone, he asked, "I'm sorry?"

The elderly man gestured behind him. "You just came off Deadman's Highway. If you ask me, that's a brave move."

"Brave?"

"Does this room have an echo?" The elderly man chuckled. "Have you not been told the stories?"

"Now, Teddy. Don't you go messing with this gentleman's head. He has no interest in listening to those foolish, outdated stories. Here's your cup of coffee," said the waitress as she placed it in front of Ron.

After witnessing a semi-truck flaming down the road, Ron was curious about what the old man had to say. "What stories? This is my first time in this part of Utah."

Carefully placing his coffee cup on the counter, Teddy's lips curved into a peculiar smile. "People claim that this road was not meant to be constructed, and that it is paved with asphalt and blood. Even this café shouldn't be here. There was some kind of land dispute. Through eminent domain, the government seized the land from a family that claimed their ancestors had been there since the first settlers."

Ron nodded his head somberly. He knew about the government's practice of appropriating land for road building, lake construction, or the establishment of new parks. "Wow, that's some bad luck."

"Bad luck for who?" Teddy gave a sarcastic chuckle. "The man that owned the land was a truck driver just like you. They say he went crazy after he and his family were made to move off the land. Without warning, he hopped into his truck and began harassing anyone who dared to use his highway."

"Whoa, that's seriously creepy." Ron thought about the ghostly truck that was on fire. "What happened to this guy?"

Teddy absentmindedly scratched his chin, feeling the roughness of his gray stubble. "Well, I heard he killed a few people by running them off the road or pushing their cars with his truck to make them wreck on that sharp curve. Word has it that he killed a family, a waitress, and an old man who had the audacity to take that road."

Ron's stomach started churning uncomfortably. "Do you know what happened to the truck driver?"

"When he found out the police were after him, he set his truck on fire. He drove down the highway until his truck was consumed." Teddy shook his head and spoke with a hint of sarcasm in his tone. "What a way to go, huh? Couldn't have happened to a better guy."

Ron asked that his food be packed up into a to-go box. His hunger had disappeared completely by that point. After thanking the waitress, he proceeded to leave. Teddy trailed closely behind him. "You should avoid taking that road again, if you ask me. You got lucky, son. He let you go."

Turning around to face Teddy, he was met with a terrifying sight. The waitress and the old man were gone, and the Cuppa Coffee café was nothing but a burned-out building. His heart hammered against his ribcage. Ron glanced at his hands and saw that he was still gripping his paper coffee cup and full a styrofoam to-go box. The world felt like it was spinning as he turned to see the sunrise peeking over the back of his parked semi-truck.

Ron hurled the food and coffee to the ground and sprinted towards his truck. As he climbed into the cab and forcefully closed the door. The only sounds that reached his ears were his strained breath and his heart thumping. First, he glanced at the side mirrors, then shifted his gaze to the front. It was just him and the dessert. It was mind-boggling to Ron that he couldn't comprehend how any of it was possible. Ghosts were not something he believed in. Yet, he was living a ghost story in real time.

Laughing to himself, Ron voiced his thoughts out loud. "I guess mom was right, strange things only happen after midnight."

Dread overwhelmed him the moment the words were spoken. After completing his delivery, he had to travel back the same way he had arrived. Didn't the old man caution him against going back that way? The truck was too large to find any alternate routes. He had no choice. Ron had to confront the Deadman's Highway once more.

Afterlife

THE QUICK OF DORIAN'S fingernails pulsed painfully. He could never break the nasty habit of chewing on his nails. In times of stress, his fingernails didn't stand a chance. Dorian kept his concerns to himself and rarely spoke about them. Throughout his life, he kept his head down and his mouth shut. Regardless of how he felt, Dorian allowed others to speak on his behalf in his job, life, and marriage. When he hit forty, he couldn't even answer simple questions about his favorite food or life ambitions. Dorian just went through life parroting how others lived their lives, ate their food, went to school and got a degree, and picked out the perfect wife. Never did he ever mention how much he hated every second of it. His wife was always pushing him to his breaking point. He felt a little guilty when he faked tears when he found out he was sterile and couldn't have children. Despite the pity from others, Dorian felt a sense of relief that he didn't have to fake being a good dad along with his other responsibilities. While his wife sobbed to her mother about their uncertain future, Dorian went to bed and enjoyed the best sleep he had experienced in their five years of marriage.

Dorian was an actor, and he was the only one that knew it. It was on his forty-first birthday when he felt a snap within him. Perhaps it was the fake smiling faces singing happy birthday to him or the five shots of vodka he drank in his closet, but a sharp pain twisted in his brain. He tried to push through and smile as if nothing bothered him like he always did, but this time, it was too much. Dorian stood, his hand flying to his brow in a sudden movement. One by one, the voices quieted. Tara placed the cake, with an absurd number of candles still lit on the table. "Darling, are you alright?"

With a shake of his head, Dorian retreated to the kitchen, escaping the astonished looks from his guest. In a frenzy, he rummaged through cabinets and drawers for painkillers. Beads of sweat trickled down his face as the throbbing pain reached excruciating levels. The feeling of Tara standing behind him made him certain that she was there, looking helpless as she typically did. She never knew what to do. All her parents taught her was how to be a housewife, nothing more. Dorian harbored resentment towards Tara and the fact he had to take care of everything while she enjoyed a princess-like existence. His brain throbbed with pent-up anger, hurt, and resentment accumulated over the years. For the first time in his life, Dorian spun around and faced Tara's doe-eyed stare. "For once in your life, stop staring and help me find the pain reliever!"

Dorian's forceful words made Tara jump. It was the first time she had ever heard a man raise his voice. Soft-spoken men seemed to be a common characteristic of her father and most of the males in her family. With trembling hands and lips, she quickly sprang into action and found the Tylenol in the cabinet next to the refrigerator. Dorian appeared somewhat deranged as he forcefully took the bottle from her. Opening the bottle, he appeared completely different from the man she married, as he consumed four pills and washed them down with water. As Tara spoke, her own voice barely reached her ears. "Dorian, can you please explain what is happening? You're not acting like yourself."

After that, darkness enveloped everything.

Dorian couldn't remember a thing. All he could recall was the fact that he had been in an accident and had a near-death encounter. Now, he had no choice but to sit through support group meetings. Like everything else in his life, someone forced him into it. Dorian surveyed the room that he had no choice but to sit in day after day. He gazed beyond the nervous expressions of the individuals seated in a circle, their eyes locked on to each other or on the floor. The room's design resembled a peaceful sanctuary, allowing an escape from the chaos of daily life, and it made you forget that you were in a hospital psychiatric ward. To promote relaxation, they painted the walls in gentle, calming shades of blue and green. The room was spacious, with enough room for the circle of chairs and a refreshment station offering coffee, snacks, and herbal teas. To give it a cozy touch of home, they added a large plush carpet. Soft instrumental music played in the background as a box of tissues sat unused in the corner.

Despite their purpose to inspire, the posters on the wall only angered Dorian. They offered words of encouragement like "You can do it" and "Don't quit." Somehow, the faces smiling in the photos looked cruel and condescending. Their expressions were devoid of joy. Dorian quickly looked away from them. Though he didn't want to admit it, he found himself relieved when the councilor entered to start the meeting. Dorian would have chosen anything over having to look at those disturbing posters.

Carrying a clipboard under his arm and a coffee in his hand, Anthony entered the room. Every day, he moved in the same way, without fail. As he glanced around the room, Anthony had a strange smile on his face and nodded politely at anyone who met his gaze. He would softly address a few people, uttering, "Great to see you, Anna. Happy you could join us, Allan." He made it look like everyone had voluntarily decided to be there. Everyone present in the loopy lodge, including Dorian, had been thrown in for different reasons. The only thing they had in common was the fact they each had a near-death experience.

One after another, the participants were asked to describe what they witnessed after dying, and Dorian waited patiently for his turn to share his story. A few people found themselves in an out-of-body state, while others reported hearing voices or seeing a tunnel of white light. Every individual appeared enthusiastic about sharing their stories, and they dedicated an entire session to discussing their experiences. Dorian didn't want to talk about his experience. It wasn't because the people there were bad. The creepy woman who never missed a meeting was to blame.

There was nothing unusual about her appearance, except for the unsettling way her eyes would focus on the patient while they spoke. Dorian couldn't quite put it into words, but even her manner of holding the notebook and jotting down every word was unnerving. There was never any explanation for her being there. Anthony would just give her a nod and continue with the meeting. Nobody else appeared to mind her presence, or the condition of her wrinkled and stained pink nurses' scrubs. Dorian was certain that the nursing cap the nurse wore had gone out of style in the 1980s. He couldn't help but notice the resemblance between her and Nurse Ratched, with her victory rolls and cat-like grin.

Once Anthony sat down, he wasted no time in searching for his list of names. "Let me see. Whose turn is it today?"

Annoyed, Dorian let out a breath and silently cursed Anthony's act. He knew well that each person had already had a turn. It appeared as though he relished the torture that everyone endured, eagerly anticipating their name to be selected in the lunatic lottery. "Ah, looks like it's Dorian's turn today."

Everyone's attention turned towards Dorian.

In an effort to ignore the nurse's unsettling gaze, Dorian cleared his throat. "Um... I'm not sure how to begin."

Anthony suppressed his typical patronizing remarks and forced a smile to show he understood. "Simply start from the beginning."

Rubbing his knee with his sore fingers, Dorian shook his head. "I don't know. It's like one minute I was in the kitchen, then suddenly there was a flash of light."

"How would you describe that light?" Anthony said eagerly.

"I have never seen a light quite like it. I know it sounds odd, but it was clean and crisp in a way that is hard to explain. My mind felt clear and pure because of it. If peace and joy had a visual representation, it would be that light. I didn't experience fear, anger, or confusion. It was a place, and a feeling all at the same time." As the remaining memories emerged, Dorian's heart started thumping.

Anthony leaned in as the nurse wrote everything he said in her notebook with a sideways grin. "What happened after the light?"

"I don't know if I want to talk anymore about it." Beads of perspiration formed on Dorian's forehead.

"Releasing this burden is essential for your progress, even though it's difficult." Anthony said as he licked his lips.

The old pressure to please others resurfaced for Dorian. It was a type of peer pressure that made him do whatever people told him to do. His heart raced and his mind swirled in strange patterns. Memories overwhelmed his mind at such a rapid pace he felt like throwing up. The words flowed out like a child confessing a wrongdoing. "The scene became dark, as if someone had flipped a switch. I felt scared and lost. The sensation of weightlessness overtook me as I floated in the air, my feet not touching the ground. It seemed like an eternity before another light emerged. It was below me. Blue and white lights were flashing. I realized after a minute that what I saw was police lights. There was a lot of chaos happening. Some people were running and yelling for an ambulance, while others were shouting at onlookers eager to catch a glimpse of the commotion."

Anthony paused while the nurse took notes before moving on to his next question. "Dorian, can you explain what was going on? Can you tell me what you saw?"

Dorian shook his head. "I don't know."

"Use your brain, Dorian. Think back. Chaos and lights unfolded beneath you. What was happening, Dorian? Think!" Anthony licked his lips again, but this time, it reminded Dorian of a snake as his tongue slipped in and out of his mouth.

Dorian glanced at the nurse. She attempted to give him a sympathetic smile. He felt shivers coursing through his body. There was a strange vibe coming from her, but he couldn't figure out what it was. For the first time since the therapy group began, she spoke. The sound of her voice was both gentle and haunting. "Come now, Dorian. You can trust us. Our primary goal is to offer help."

Something in the way she looked at him made him feel like he was being hypnotized. The floodgates opened, and everything he tried to conceal spilled out, as if she had given him a truth serum. His eyes teared up as his words poured out of his mouth. What came out surprised even him. "I do not know how much time I spent hovering over the scene. Amidst the commotion of people crying, shouting, and issuing commands, I realized it was a horrific car accident when I saw the mangled pieces of metal scattered around."

"Tell me, what else did you see?" asked the nurse in her soothing tone.

"The entire area was drenched in blood. I..." Dorian tried to break his eye contact with the nurse, but it was of no use. "I followed the trail of blood, and I saw a car wrapped around a tree. It was terrible. Firefighters arrived at the scene and used the jaws of life to remove the car's roof. Someone was trapped inside the car."

"Dorian," Anthony asked, standing up, "Who was the person trapped in the car?" He was no longer hiding the fact he was excited to hear the terrible details.

Remembering his disheveled state, with blood trickling down his forehead, Dorian's hands shook as he admitted, "It was me."

With every last detail documented in her notebook, the nurse neatly stowed her pen in her shirt pocket. Laughter bubbled from her flawlessly painted pink lips. "That was fun," she remarked, abandoning the innocent accent she had used with Dorian.

Dorian regained control, and a surge of anger brewed. He was exhausted by this place, with no energy remaining. "Fun? This is your idea of fun?"

The nurse grinned with amusement at Dorian. "If you have been in this business as long as I have, you would think this is better than taking candy from a baby."

Dorian looked around the room. The rest of the patients shifted uncomfortably, exchanging confused expressions with the others sitting next to them. Heat permeated the air, making it feel thick, while a low hum filled the room. Anthony's appearance had drastically changed from a hospital counselor to a deranged animal. Struggling to suppress his amusement, he dropped the clipboard.

The soothing music playing in the background skipped like an old vinyl record, while the calming atmosphere became dark and foreboding. Something wasn't right. Dorian stood up and approached Anthony. "Why are you laughing?" Anthony's laughter sounded more menacing as it grew louder.

Dorian's rage manifested in a forceful punch to Anthony's face. Panicked, the patients vacated their metal seats in the nick of time to watch Anthony slide across the floor while knocking over the chairs like bowling pins. Anthony's laughter only escalated. Dorian was on the verge of walking over to Anthony to complete what he had started, but sharp fingernails dug into his shoulder and forcefully spun him around. In front of him stood a nurse who seemed unhinged. Her lips formed a sneer as her nurse's cap tumbled to the floor. Protruding from her forehead were small horns and her eyes, green and watery, seemed pale. "Not so fast, Dorian. You're going nowhere."

Never had Dorian experienced such intense hatred and fear towards someone as he did in this moment. No matter how much he struggled, punched, or screamed, she refused to let go. "Let me go!"

"Settle down, Dorian. If I set you free, I'll miss out on the joy of unveiling the rest of your story. Look!" The nurses' eyes bore into Dorians' soul. The events leading up to his blackout unfolded like scenes from a movie. Dorian witnessed the shock on everyone's faces as he abruptly rose from his birthday celebration, clutching his head in pain, and flipped the table before storming away to the kitchen. Watching Tara chase after him shattered his heart into countless pieces. Dorian witnessed his own outburst as his innocent bride's face twisted in pain as he snatched the Tylenol from her hands.

Despite his shouting, Tara maintained her usual gentle tone when speaking to him. "Dorian, can you please explain what is happening? You're not acting like yourself," she said as she reached out and touched his shoulder.

Dorian watched in horror as he balled up his fist, spun around, and punched Tara in the face. Several things happened at once. Tara's small body twirled like a drunken ballerina. She lost her footing and her foot slipped out from underneath her. In her descent, she made a futile effort to grasp Dorian's hand, but it was too late. Tara's head made contact with the corner of the white marble counter. It played in slow motion. Dorian saw the light leave Tara's eyes. Trembling, he uttered a single word, "No."

"Oh, yessssss." The nurse hissed.

Attendees of the birthday party hurried over to see what was happening. Dorian's face displayed a twisted expression of pure evil, and everyone was a witness. Completely unrecognizable, he spat on the floor before abruptly leaving the house. "That isn't me."

"No doubt about it, it's you. Watch what happens next. It's the highlight." The nurse couldn't help but giggle with a squeaky sound this time.

The scenery in front of Dorian changed. Overwhelmed by fear, he saw himself enter his car and accelerate onto the dark highway. His corvette reached speeds he had never driven before. Dorian barreled down the interstate, taking swigs from a bottle of vodka. The sight of blue lights behind him triggered Dorian's rebellious side, causing him to let out an excited yell and veer off the interstate onto a back road. Dorian turned up the radio as the police closely pursued him, matching his every move.

The pursuit came to a terrifying end when the electric blue corvette crashed into a tree. "That's not me. It can't be," Dorian said as the therapy room came back into focus.

The nurse flung Dorian down and took pleasure in watching him crawl away on his hands and knees. "This is my favorite part of the therapy session, when you all find out the meaning of it all."

Dorian could feel the others crowding around him as they clung to each other for comfort. "What meaning? Why are you doing this?" he shouted.

"You brought this upon yourself, little boy! You murdered your wife! Then you wrapped yourself around the closest tree. For what? Was little boy blue incapable of becoming a grown man?" The patients trembled as the nurse's gaze fell on each of them, one by one. "You have all forgotten you were the worst of the worst." The nurse stood up straight, towering over Dorian. "Ladies and gentlemen, the moment you've been waiting for has arrived - the grand finale. Your purpose is not to share stories about your close encounters with death. None of you had a near-death experience, none of you survived!"

Dorian's realization left him feeling cold. He could not recall his walk to the meetings or how he arrived. As he glanced around, the walls vanished, and darkness engulfed him. Screams from all directions surrounded him. "No!"

As the nurse vanished, Dorian caught her voice one last time. "Welcome to the afterlife."

Dorian's torment had just begun.

The End

THE MORNING FOG DRIFTED across the freshly paved black-top, sprinkling mist on the windshield. The winding roads of Oregon captivated Arthur as he headed towards the cabin rented by his wife, Clare. Writer's block was clouding his mind, and it didn't help that his three kids, all under the age of ten, were on a fall break from school. Guilt consumed Arthur for leaving Clare with three energetic kids. The situation seemed unfair since she was the one in most need of a vacation, yet he was the one getting it. Clare believed in his work and wanted to support him in the only way she knew how. Arthur had never encountered writer's block until now, leaving him clueless about how to get his creative flow back. According to his agent, writer's block is like an impacted bowel. You can try to squeeze one out but, in the end, if you don't relax and let nature take its course, it'll kill you. Both Arthur's agent and his analogy were crude, but he got the point. During their last phone conversation, Tom informed him that the publisher expected to review four chapters soon, otherwise, they would assess the contract - so no pressure. The money that had been advanced for the book was already used up, and the humiliating idea of having to admit to his publisher that he couldn't repay them was giving him a migraine.

A wave of anxiety made Arthur's chest constrict. He had a plethora of story ideas scribbled in notebooks, and his ongoing book was no different. It was a story he had thought of when he was in college before he met his wife. During that time, Arthur's creativity soared, and he experienced a flood of book ideas day and night. Ideas would come to him in unexpected moments - in the shower, while driving, or even while making out with a hot chick. The ideas came so quickly that he needed to keep a small notepad in his back pocket to write them down. Once he got married, his attention shifted towards cookouts, parties, anniversaries, pregnancies, and then something unimaginable happened. Arthur felt his eyes stinging as he rolled his window down. A rush of frosty morning air swept over his face and dried his tears. Once his mother passed away, he had trouble composing anything longer than a paragraph. Arthur would often find himself lost in thought, not knowing how he ended up in various locations in the house. One minute he would be writing, and the next he would be standing in front of the refrigerator, door open, studying what was inside, yet he lacked any hunger or thirst.

For almost two years, the publisher was understanding, until the demand for another Arthur Nightingale book became impossible to ignore. Arthur found amusement in the drastic change he experienced, going from an unknown person juggling three jobs to becoming a sought-after author. Despite trying his best, he couldn't write another book. Arthur would write an entire short story, and every time Clare read it, she would comment on how dark it was, even for him, and how it lacked an ending. The enjoyment of being a horror writer faded when sadness entered his life, robbing him of a piece of his soul. A huge part of him felt as if it were inside the coffin with his mother. He couldn't shake the sadness no matter what he tried. Explaining it to everyone required words he didn't have. How does a writer, whose profession revolves around words, explain their voice has been silenced?

Arthur's inability to write endings to his stories was the most painful aspect of losing his mother; it felt like a representation of his heartbreak. After he recovered from the initial shock of his mother's sudden death, everyone assumed he would resume his life within a year. Arthur couldn't understand why everyone universally accepted a year as the appropriate length of time for grieving. After being together for forty years, he had to stop grieving for his mother's loss after just one year. It was an impossible expectation.

Arthur ended up spending an entire week on the couch, engrossed in one sitcom after another, without eating, sleeping, showering, or speaking to anyone. The weight of grief became too much for him to bear while maintaining his normal routine. The emptiness that lingered had manifested into a corporeal presence, overpowering his body. It was as if he was an observer in a movie theater in his mind, watching his life unfold. Clare seized the remote and shut off the TV. Arthur had the odor of a dirty sock and appeared homeless, causing Clare to reach her breaking point. "Arthur, this has crossed a line, and it's become too much. I've reached my limit and can't watch this any further. I know you're grieving the loss of your mother, and I won't pretend to fully grasp the magnitude of that sorrow since I haven't experienced it myself." Clare laid her hand on her chest. She felt emotionally drained after talking to him like this. Clare had the patience of a saint and a soft-spoken nature. Arthur knew he had pushed her too far. Clare never had a conversation with him that lacked emotion. As the words flowed, her face remained calm and expressionless. "We loved her too, Arthur, but life is moving on and you are not. The kids need you... I need you."

Clare had the cabin booked, and a bag packed before Arthur could come up with an acceptable argument that she would buy. She planted a quick goodbye kiss on his lips, preventing any protests, and equipped him with the cabin's location on his phone as she ushered him out the door. Now, he found himself barreling down a wet back road in the beautiful state of Oregon. Evergreen trees surrounded Arthur on both sides of the narrow road, their branches extending towards him like a warm embrace. The rain falling on the roof of his car merged seamlessly with the road and the engine's calming hum. As he drove deeper into the heart of Oregon's rugged landscape, Arthur heard his map chime. "In a quarter of a mile, turn right."

Following the instructions, Arthur found himself on a narrow dirt road that was rapidly becoming a muddy path. His Subaru Outback's four-wheel drive and traction control came to the rescue when his tires started slipping in the slick muck. For the first time in months, Arthur felt a surge of excitement. Arthur, like many writers, found joy in embarking on thrilling adventures and discovering unexplored territories to spark creativity. As he drove, he imagined a character lost in the woods. Constructing a backstory with horror elements, Arthur imagined encountering new monsters at every corner. The potential outcomes were limitless.

When the car reached the last bend, the phone gave its final chime. "You have reached your destination."

Amongst the towering trees, a rustic cabin awaited his presence. The owner, in anticipation of his arrival, must've prepared the cabin. It was more primitive than Arthur had expected. In fact, it appeared that no one had occupied the place in quite some time. The exterior appeared aged and battered, with wooden surfaces showing signs of wear and tear like scratches, dents, wood bee holes, lichen, and moss. Arthur was relieved to see the roof was metal at least- everyone knew metal roofs would last until doomsday. A gentle glow emanated from the grimy windows, while a crooked stone chimney jutted out of the slanted roof, spewing out smoke.

Arthur took in the view of the forested surroundings. It was the most intense déjà vu he had ever felt. The trees, shrubs, rocks, and the sound of the nearby stream were all familiar. Arthur disregarded it as either a coincidence or a potential scenario where Clare had shown him the cabin, as he retrieved the bag she had packed from the car. When Arthur got to the door, he noticed there wasn't a pin pad for entering a code to get in. Instead of panicking about not having a code or key, Arthur tried the door and discovered, to his surprise, that it was unlocked.

As he entered, the inviting warmth and the scent of aged wood and hearth smoke enveloped him. The cabin's inside was a stark contrast to its outside appearance. From the exterior, the cabin appeared aged and neglected, but the interior was pristine and welcoming. Fire crackled in the hearth, casting a soft glow as flickering lanterns illuminated the cabin. A neatly arranged snug blanket on the brown leather couch beckoned someone to enjoy a cup of hot cocoa. Glancing around the room, Arthur's eyes fell upon a bookcase brimming with well-worn but beloved books. A loft above was accessible by a narrow staircase, where Arthur could see a bed made with a heavy patchwork quilt turned down for his bedtime.

Arthur turned his attention to the corner of the room. A nineteen seventies cream colored Olympia traveler typewriter sat on a desk with a stack of white paper. It was the same typewriter Arthur used during his college days. While the trust fund babies had the newest computers, Arthur pounded out his papers on an Olympia special he found at a garage sale. Despite the ridicule he received, Arthur had the highest grades in his creative writing classes. It now sat there, waiting for him like an old friend. "Clare thought of everything," Arthur said to no one.

"Clare must've thought the typewriter would inspire an ending to my story." Arthur thought to himself as he closed the door behind him and dropped his bag on the floor. In the cabin, he felt as though time had come to a standstill. It was odd to him that, even though he didn't see any cars passing on the narrow driveway, the cabin felt as if someone had been there.

Arthur's lips were dry, but he didn't feel thirsty for water. No matter how hard he looked, Arthur couldn't find any alcohol in the refrigerator or cabinets. He despised admitting it, but warm bourbon helped him relax and it opened his mind. *"This is Clare's doing; she hates the fact I need a drink. A small glass is all I need, not a lot."* Regret consumed Arthur as he noticed the hatred in his thoughts towards his wife. Clare was a good woman, but Arthur felt she would never grasp his struggle to write a novel, especially while in pain.

Clare was annoyingly perfect, as was the family she came from. The Walker family had money- lots of money. Arthur only witnessed them drinking on special occasions, such as weddings, engagement parties, or graduations. The Nightingale family was the family you never wanted living next door to you. Arthur's father guzzled beer like it was water, while his mother turned a blind eye. Everyone in the family had to deal with it and his father didn't care. It was only after his father's death from the cirrhosis of the liver that they found peace. Arthur never cried; he felt relieved.

Without his Kentucky Bourbon, Arthur couldn't write a single word. He carried the burden of his father's alcoholic curse and attempted, with little success, to hide the shame it brought. In a swift motion, Arthur grabbed his keys and left without stopping to unwind. Mindful of the icy-like conditions, Arthur drove his Subaru carefully on the muddy drive-way. Arthur found a nearby town called Troutperch Lake; it was small, but it had to have a liquor store.

A lingering dampness, heavy and cold, hung over Trout-perch. Even the old buildings seemed to huddle together, trying to keep warm. The streets were wet, and a dense fog blurred the edges of town, making it look as if it were a barrier. Arthur parked his car on the street in front of a bustling café, where people were sitting inside, trying to stay warm and dry. A waitress holding a coffee carafe waved to him as she flashed her wide, toothy grin. Arthur gave a small nod before turning around to find what he was looking for. The only shops he could see had nothing to do with alcohol. While there were many fishing and outdoor shops, there was a lack of liquor stores. Arthur's brow glistened with perspiration. In order to finish his book, he needed a drink. Anything would do. At this point, he would take a beer, a glass of wine, or a shot of moonshine.

Once again, Arthur turned around and, this time, the wait-ress beckoned him inside. Figuring the waitress would know how to find a store that sold bourbon, Arthur walked inside. A sudden silence enveloped the café. With a smile, the waitress waved. The name tag she was wearing read, "Hello, call me Sandy." Sporting bright pink gum and sparkling blue eyes, Sandy placed a menu before him, patting a stool with her milky white hand. "Come on, Arthur, have a seat."

Startled, Arthur's eyes darted around the room. Everyone was staring at him. He glanced at Sandy, who gave the waiting stool one more pat. "Have we met before?"

"Everyone knows who you are, Arthur. Now, be a good boy and have a seat."

Arthur decided Sandy and the others knew him from his bestselling books, or someone squealed that he would be there working on a book. Either way, Arthur was hoping he would not be disturbed by a crazed fan. After witnessing writers being assaulted by self-proclaimed number one fans, Arthur made a promise to himself to avoid a similar outcome. As he sat on the stool, Sandy poured him a cup of coffee. "Thank you," he mumbled.

The way Sandy kept smiling at him made him feel uneasy. "I'm sorry if I've been staring at you. It's just great to see you again."

"I believe there's a case of mistaken identity here. This is my first time in Troutperch," Arthur replied, confused.

With equal confusion, Sandy scanned the room before facing Arthur again. "Well, it has been a while since you were here last. I suppose our faces are forgettable if you think about it. I suppose small town folks are like background actors in a movie."

A shiver ran down Arthur's arms. "Faces can slip my mind, sure, but a place called Troutperch?" He chuckled. "I think you might be thinking about a different person. That's easy to do. I'm staying at..."

"At the Tillman cabin, you're working on a book. Yeah, that's where you always stay and you come into town and ask where the liquor store is," Sandy interrupted with a giggle as she smoothed out her hair with her fingertips. While she continued to babble, Arthur noticed stains that resembled droplets of blood on her apron. "And that's when I remind you that in Troutperch, it's a dry county." Arthur couldn't ignore the stiff and robotic tone in Sandy's voice as she spoke. Her delivery was rehearsed, and it felt like she was reading from a script.

A sense of unease filled Arthur. Although he couldn't remember Troutperch or its inhabitants, they behaved as though they knew him. He felt a surge of anxiety, causing his chest to rise and fall rapidly as he backed out of the café. Sandy had a strange smile on her face as she waved for him to come back in. Arthur politely waved her away and turned to walk around town. Nothing looked familiar. No matter where he went, he couldn't escape the feeling that people recognized him, and constant waves of déjà vu haunted him. *"Surely I have seen this place on television or Clare showed me this in a magazine,"* Arthur thought to himself as he headed for his car. Before he started feeling like he had gone crazy, he had to go home.

Climbing into his Subaru, Arthur swiftly made a U-turn. As he drove by, he couldn't help but notice the pale-faced individuals peering out of the windows of each building, leaving him uncertain if his eyes were playing tricks on him. Each of them gave him a cold and vacant expression.

Construction signs, dense fog, and rusty cars blocked every road out of town. The only route that was clear was the path leading back to the cabin. Arthur was determined to put some space between himself and Troutperch, so he retraced his steps along the winding roads and down the muddied driveway. As soon as he returned, the cabin greeted him with its familiar and comforting sight - windows aglow and smoke rising from the chimney.

A tormenting silence met him as he opened his car door and made his way into the cabin. He focused his gaze on the typewriter on the desk. Someone had placed a piece of paper inside the typewriter and placed a glass of Kentucky bourbon next to it, with the bottle sitting beside it. Arthur was positive that he had spotted just one set of footprints in the mud outside, which were made by him going back and forth, and he was certain that there was no alcohol present when he first got there. Nevertheless, there it was, the familiar muse he knew and cherished so much. Arthur looked around the cabin. "Someone here?" The only response he got was the crackling sound coming from the fireplace.

Arthur moved towards the writing desk. The paper inside the typewriter had words written on it. *"Complete the story and you're free to go. The End will save you."*

"Alright, who's playing with me?" Arthur asked as he spun around to face the living room. He felt panic building up in his throat.

Dread filled the air as Arthur listened to the typewriter behind him awaken and begin typing its reply. Driven by morbid curiosity, he turned around to read the paper. *"You are playing with you. Finish any story you like and then you can go."*

Arthur felt as if his mind was slipping away. "Who are you?" he asked. He anxiously watched as the black, rounded keys typed on their own.

"I am you."

Arthur's body jolted as he realized that he was sitting in the chair, with his hands suspended over the keys. The glass, which was full only moments ago, was now empty, as was the half-drunk bottle of bourbon. The chair fell onto the floor with a deafening thud as he stood. Arthur whirled around to look at the room behind him in the cabin. Previously a source of happiness, the fireplace now appeared devoid of life, with a cold and dull appearance. With its folded blanket, the couch no longer had a welcoming appearance. The leather appeared dirty, and the blanket showed signs of wear. The upstairs bed, adorned with a cozy patterned quilt, looked as if someone had carelessly tossed the blanket on the floor. The cabin was illuminated solely by the glowing lantern on the desk.

When Arthur looked down, he realized his chair was surrounded by balled-up paper. Arthur bent down and grabbed one; it was about a haunted lake. He took hold of another one; it was a story about a woman being frozen and awakened in the future. Numerous papers contained incomplete short stories on topics like time travel, ghosts, hallucinations, and even an unused tale about a small-town deranged waitress who served up a human barbecue. The one about going to hell scared him the most. Arthur couldn't remember writing them at all.

"How long have I been here?" Arthur asked himself as he clumsily navigated past the overturned chair, opened the front door, and stepped onto the porch. The intensity of the rain made it nearly impossible for him to see the trees surrounding the porch. It felt like something, or someone, was trying to trap him in the small cabin. Arthur rushed back in and made sure to close the door behind him. "Is someone here with me? Who's doing this?"

The clicking and clacking of the typewriter started up again. Arthur walked over to take a look at the paper. *"This is a nightmare, or I've lost my mind," Arthur thought with terror as he stood looking down at his beloved typewriter. Shaking his head in a slow back-and-forth sweep of denial, he thought to himself, "Someone must be playing a game with me, or I gave myself alcohol poisoning, like Clare told me would happen. Why did I take off on her like that? She deserves better than me." Arthur jumped back.*

With a quick glance around the room, Arthur raised his voice. "Stop doing this to me!"

The typewriter wrote in unison as Arthur yelled. *"Stop doing this to me!"*

"What are you?" Arthur asked, his breathing becoming slow and shallow.

"What are you?" The typewriter waited for Arthur to speak again.

There was something the typewriter wanted from Arthur, and he could sense it. "What do you want?"

"What do you want? You want to finish the story. You need to write a story and end it with, The End."

A wave of pain engulfed Arthur's chest. "I can't; I've tried and failed every time. It's too much."

"If you write it, you can be free. Your short stories are the key to your escape."

Arthur closed his eyes; the memories came flooding back to him. He began writing a book of short stories and drank excessively, leading Clare to become angry and cry during their confrontation. With his heart pounding, Arthur recalled how he had stormed out of the house in a drunken rage. The keys to his Subaru poked him in the pocket and, foolishly, he climbed in behind the wheel and took off down the road. With no sense of direction, he navigated the bewildering road, distorted by the haze of bourbon. The last memory he had was of himself being airborne and seeing tree limbs coming through the glass. Both the cabin and the town were figments of his imagination. Arthur could feel himself hanging upside down in his car seat as his seatbelt kept him from certain death.

Arthur looked down at the typewriter. "Is this the end for me?"

"Not yet. You are hanging on. Finish your story and maybe we can crawl to safety."

Arthur picked up the overturned chair, sat down, took a deep breath and exhaled before stretching out his fingers. He placed them on the keys and started typing.

THE END.

About the author

B. D. West is a captivating fiction author known for her diverse writing style across genres. Her writing spans across various genres, including paranormal fiction, science fiction, fantasy fiction, thrillers, poetry, and crime fiction. B. D. West is the author of Wynter of Wolves, Wynter of Wolves The Seven, The Dark of October, and The Veil.

B. D. West was born in Nashville, TN. Until the age of 17, she called Tennessee home before joining her mother in the Appalachian Mountains of North Carolina. The people living in the small towns of the Appalachian Mountains, North Carolina, and The Easter Band of the Cherokee have been a constant source of inspiration for her short stories and characters.

After being given a writing assignment in 9th grade by her English teacher, Mrs. Smithson, B. D. West has been writing since the age of 14. Writing has been both a passion and a source of comfort for her, spanning over 30 years, as she navigated through numerous challenges. When her son Dakota was 5, he was diagnosed with Asperger Syndrome. Using social stories, B found that her love for writing became her most effective teaching tool for him. Despite developing an autoimmune disorder and fibromyalgia, she kept her dream alive by composing poetry, and stories for her son. She also wrote letters to the editor for local newspapers, and articles for the Autism Society of NC support group chapter of which she was the chapter president for almost 5 years. In 2020, her debut book, Wynter of Wolves, was released.

In addition to being a writer, B. D. West enjoys reading, nature walks, indie music, traveling, movies, and quality time with loved ones.

B. resides with her husband Eric, son Dakota, two bossy cats named Ruth and Idgie, and their chihuahua Bandit in North Carolina.